DESPICABLE

By
Timothy Bryan

Copyright © 2022 by Timothy Bryan

All rights reserved. No part of this publication may be reproduced, distributed, or transmitted in any form whatsoever or by any means (electronic, mechanical, photocopying, recording, or otherwise), or stored in a database or retrieval system without the prior written permission of both the copyright owner and the above publisher, except as permitted under the U.S. Copyright Act of 1976 or for the inclusion quotations in an acknowledged review.

First published in the United States 2022
Printed in the United States of America

"Do not act as if you will live 10,000 years. Death hangs over you. While you live, while it is in your power, be good."
-**Marcus Aurelius**

Table of Contents

Chapter One 7
Chapter Two 17
Chapter Three 33
Chapter Four 59
Chapter Five 71
Chapter Six 85
Chapter Seven 97
Chapter Eight 115
Chapter Nine 127
Chapter Ten 141
Chapter Eleven 153
Chapter Twelve 175
Chapter Thirteen 187
Chapter Fourteen 203
Chapter Fifteen 211
Chapter Sixteen 225
Chapter Seventeen 237
Chapter Eighteen 253
About the Author 259

Chapter One

Western Front, France - 1916

Explosions of artillery blasts resound in the distance, illuminating a dark skyline above the tortured hilly fields of Northern France. Orange blossoms of impacting artillery rounds burst in the distance, causing a jarring backdrop to the field of battle, and making it hard to determine the precise location of each detonating munition.

Because the explosions are some distance away from friendly trenches, that they are felt so close to allied forces is significant—they're of high caliber and meant to obliterate the enemy. Screeching rounds of deadly salvos continually arc towards the German adversary, surely causing them extensive casualties in their fortified redoubts.

To the near side of the front lines are a series of snaking trenches, and they streak in various directions, twisting like earthen tentacles towards the rear of allied

DESPICABLE

lines. Crouching soldiers scamper back and forth amongst the channeled soil, attending to their duties while trying to avoid the death that hovers over the stifling war zone.

Private Thomas Biddle trudges through one of the muddy and dank pathways, ducking as low as his spindly frame will allow. His youthful face is scared under the night's flashing lights, and he struggles to control his breathing as he processes his fear. Though some distance from the immediate front, an errant counter-battery round from the enemy artillery could find him at any time, ending his brief stay on earth.

Dying at such an industrial scale in the First World War means such random deaths are common, and Thomas is well aware he won't be missed if that happens. He's already forgotten the names of many fellow soldiers that preceded him in death, usually without finding much of their bodies to bury afterward.

Stopping for a rest, Thomas takes a moment to collect his thoughts. When he sneaks a glance over the parapet, he sees only distant flashes of stray lights and coils of smoke over the battered area of No-Man's Land. Phalanxes of barbed wired stretch into that murky environment, as if they're signposts leading the way towards a distant and foreboding destiny.

Lowering his head, Thomas removes his helmet and rubs his close-shaved hair with a frustrated sigh. He knows he's not truly cut out for this type of work, and he

CHAPTER ONE

hopes for the war and his place in it to soon come to an end. It wasn't long ago when he was kicking the soccer ball around with his brothers, hoping to get a position at the local football club. Now, it seems half of the boys he grew up with are dead or injured, while the other half may soon join them.

Replacing his head cover, Thomas contemplates the future while he tries to avoid hyperventilating. When he enlisted as a volunteer a year earlier, it had been in a show of fierce patriotism, as well as a desire to curry favor with hosts of adoring girls from his hometown of Birmingham. Now, the idea seems like the quaint action of a mad and foolish boy, one who would be better served by returning home and living a peaceful life eating his mother's delicious cooking.

Sighing, Thomas focuses ahead and sprints to the next trench, where his gaze falls upon the headquarters' dugout. To either side of its sandbagged entrance stands an armed man, each holding a bolt-action rifle at the ready. Their grim expressions show no inclination towards kindness as they peer at him.

Thomas paces toward the bunker, flashing a smile and a scrap of paper as he enters the dusty confines of the reinforced command area. Being a messenger in a war environment is not a long-lived profession, but it does allow for going where you are sent without restriction. He ducks down as he enters, letting his eyes adjust to the cramped interior of the British Forces Headquarters' Unit.

Inside, the headquarters area is a tidy affair, considering its location and purpose. Chairs and a large table fight for space with officers and assistants going about their duty of administering a battle. Thomas moves his gaze about, looking for the target of his message.

Standing near several charts at a far wall, Colonel Patterson stares up at numerous units marked on the smudged contours of a strategic map. He is a balding and pudgy man in his forties, who from a distance could be mistaken for a commonplace clerk in any stodgy firm in London. Closer up, however, his steely demeanor and piercing eyes show a committed and icy professional, one who is rigidly attentive to his job.

Glancing over, Patterson notices Thomas, who seems lost in the sea of the headquarters' staff.

"Well, what do you have, Private?" Patterson asks, his tone and bearing becoming impatient. "We haven't the whole war to wait for you."

Thomas nods and scurries forward, holding out his note with a shaking hand.

Patterson softens his expression at the sight of the trembling soldier and gently takes the message. Withdrawing reading glasses from a pocket, he sets the spectacles on his bulbous nose. As he reads the crinkled paper, his demeanor grows worried, and he rubs his fingers over his scant mustache in a nervous gesture.

CHAPTER ONE

Glancing up, Patterson dismisses Thomas, who looks elated to be set free. Thomas departs the bunker entrance with a perfunctory salute, rushing back out amongst the loud and dangerous trenches.

Breathing deep, Patterson collects himself and walks determinedly from the room. He paces ahead through several dim tunnels, where dust puffs from the ceiling in concert with the distant artillery explosions.

Patterson walks past another guard, nodding at the rigid soldier as he makes his way into a small office. The room is filled with communication equipment set upon a sturdy table, with all manner of radios and telephones filling up its surface. A single light bulb dangles from the ceiling, gently swaying with the insistent detonations of the far-off battle. Two soldiers are perched on chairs in front of it, talking into headsets with hushed tones.

Patterson leans down to speak into the ear of one of the men, keeping his voice low.

"Well, this is it, Lieutenant," says Patterson. "We are a go for zero six hundred. May God have mercy on those poor bastards' souls."

The Lieutenant, a young man with an oily complexion, looks up at Patterson. His face is stern, but his features are mixed with a worried mess of contrasting emotions. Gulping, he merely nods at the colonel.

#

DESPICABLE

Deep in the confines of the ground below the headquarters, another dusty room is occupied by two soldiers. Lamps hanging on the walls provide illumination to the dark area, throwing shadows around the underground space.

In this place, there are soil-hewn walls and a gaggle of wires running along the floors. Like some bizarre spider web, the cluster of mismatched cables exit the room in all directions.

At a table in the middle of the primitive room sit Sergeant Blakeley and Corporal Evans. Seated across from one another, each stares ahead with a worried grimace, like they're unsure if they should be there. Glancing down, they focus on two detonators on the crude tabletop. Wires run from the simple electrical initiators, joining the jumble of connections on the walls and floor.

Blakely holds up a pocket watch, staring at its cloudy face in the dim light. The time is 5:59, with the second hand ticking its way towards the top of the hour. Blakely is well into middle age, but his furrowed and sweaty brow make him look older still, as if the impending events are accelerating his slide into advanced age.

Corporal Evans watches him from the other side of the table, his younger face a combination of boisterous youthfulness and trepidation. As the watch ticks ever closer to its goal, Evans' eyes flit from it to the initiator. He licks his lips, anticipating what comes next.

CHAPTER ONE

Nodding, Blakely grabs one of the detonators, and he motions for Evans to grasp the other. When the timepiece reaches its predetermined mark, the soldiers twist the plungers in precise coordination.

A cacophonous and dreadful explosion shakes the room, roiling it for an extended time. Dust sifts down from the ceiling, and for a worrying moment, the soldiers fear the area will collapse upon them. The magnitude of the eruption is fierce and frightening, as if hell itself has decided to unleash its traumatizing vengeance on the world.

After some time, the sounds and dust die down, and the room resumes its formerly calm appearance. Evans has an exhilarated expression, and he glances triumphantly up to Blakely, hoping for his excitement to be mirrored in his companion. A superficial grin crosses Evans' face.

As the choking air clears, Blakely meets Evans' gaze, but it isn't elation that the younger man sees in the Sergeant; instead, it's crushing sadness.

#

Wisps of acrid smoke drift up the ridgeline, partially obscuring the heights of numerous hills in the otherwise calm and frosty morning. The churned and broken soil that surrounds the base of the ascending terrain is marred by upturned foliage and scattered barbed wire.

DESPICABLE

Cast throughout the field below the higher ground are a multitude of bodies and broken equipment. Limbs and portions of decomposing soldiers are draped among the shell holes and husks of shattered trees in the apocalyptic scene.

The blood and dark soil in the shredded uniforms of the deceased make it difficult to determine which color of soldierly clothing they wore. Appropriate for their common end in the violent backdrop, the dead are now part of the same brotherhood of fallen warriors, without need for patriotism or nationality.

A squad of ten British soldiers carefully picks its way through the landscape. Stepping gingerly to avoid noise or detection, they approach the bottom of a misty hill, one that was recently swarming with their enemies.

Corporal Henderson peers up into the early day's light, an apprehensive scowl dominating his face. He is a fit fellow with sharp eyes, intent on surviving his stint on the front lines. He focuses into the shrouding mist and gestures for his men to begin the long advance up the precarious terrain.

Behind him, his men are equally cautious, and they swivel their heads and rifles, ready to engage any potential enemies as they trudge over the slippery grass and sharp rocks. Their advance is slow and methodical as they work their way through the swirling fog and up the steep, sodden ground.

CHAPTER ONE

Ahead, the haze partially drifts aside to allow for an orderly view of the top of the hill. Henderson stops abruptly, leveling his Lee Enfield rifle at a series of figures facing them.

A trench runs along the top of the ridge, facing out over the advancing soldiers in a perfect defensive position. Situated in the recess of their ditch stand fifteen German soldiers, upright and staring uselessly into the morning sun. The mining operation has upended the entirety of their defending breastworks, crushing them where they stand and leaving their corpses to stand watch over the advancing allied soldiers.

Henderson lowers his weapon and motions to the macabre sight.

"Poor buggers," Henderson says. "They never saw the end coming."

Each of his soldiers nods, panning to stare individually at the dead men. The solemnity of the occasion doesn't last long, however, and Henderson quickly motions for them to proceed farther into the advance. One by one, they pass the remains of the German trench, leaving the upright corpses behind as they advance farther into enemy lines.

Soon, the British soldiers have moved past the grim ditch and are lost from sight, fading into the ever-present fog that shrouds this region. The burgeoning day is again quiet after their passing.

Suddenly, at the far end of the ditch, one of the dead men begins to move. Strangely, his body begins to squirm about, as if he has learned a new dance in the loose soil. The bizarre shuffling of the crushed soldier continues for some time.

Except, the man is still dead, and his body begins to crack and gyrate with some strange force. With the rending of flesh and the cracking of his bones, the German is pulled into the earth, disappearing entirely into the fractured soil.

Down the line of the former trench, the same process is repeated for many of the other dead men. In succession, several more are yanked into the earth, their bodies disappearing under the trench system after partaking in the same shuffle of death.

In time, only a few cold men are left to continue their lifeless overwatch of the remote French countryside.

Chapter Two

Reno, Nevada - Present Day

The bright casino is lively and loud in the late evening hours. Crowds of boisterous gamblers shout throughout the gaming area as they try to overcome prodigious mathematical odds, while other celebrants focus on getting drunk as they enjoy subsidized alcohol from always-open bars to the side of the expansive gaming pits and tables.

Nods and smiling faces fill the smoky air of the raucous establishment, creating an addictive and entertaining ambiance. Most of the smiles are from booze-induced drunkenness, but the environment is nevertheless friendly, provided one has the money and inclination to play.

At a noisy craps' table, an edgy gamer throws his dice, then screams at the results in broken dismay. Elsewhere, players at various other tables recoil at the turn of an

DESPICABLE

unlucky card or the clack of a roulette ball falling into the wrong slot.

The chaotic scene is bankruptcy writ large, where predetermined negative outcomes are sold to aspiring players as their chance to gain wealth—and have fun doing it. As with all easy promises, the results are usually less pleasant.

Banks of slot machines angle in every direction, and flashing signs of huge dollar figures promise jackpots to the pensioners and working-class people who roam near the beeps and whistles of the slots. Unfortunately, these are the players least equipped to absorb financial losses in pursuit of a big payday, and far-way stares from newly destitute gamblers are distressingly common.

At one particular slot machine, far removed from the busy mobs, a young woman stares at the stopped reels of her machine. Kalisa Kinigi stews in emotions of shame and anger as her eyes lock on the credit total, which reads *0*.

Kalisa is in her mid-thirties, black, and attractive, but she has the demeanor of someone who doesn't hold back when she enjoys something. In the case of slot machines, that's not a virtue.

"Shit," Kalisa says, and she leans closer to the brightly colored screen, as if doing so will make her missing credits return.

Kalisa smacks the slot several times, punctuating each slap with a throaty curse.

CHAPTER TWO

"Fuck...fuck...fuck...fuck."

To her side, an old lady gives Kalisa a disapproving frown, wriggling her aged nose at the explosion of vulgar language. Kalisa drops her gaze from the woman, plumbing new depths of embarrassment as she digs her wallet from her purse.

When she's rewarded with an empty cash compartment, Kalisa lowers her head and pinches the bridge of her nose with her fingers. *Fuck, not again. It's the same, every time. I'm such an idiot.*

Kalisa raises her eyes to scan the casino, acting as if her losses were expected. Collecting her player's card from the machine, she heads to the ATM, which lies close to a crowd of people near the cashier's cage.

Waiting her turn at the cash machine, Kalisa looks enviously to the side at a grinning fat man with a rack of thousand-dollar chips. The man stands close to the VIP window of the cashier area, gloating with a contented and self-important expression. The high roller enjoys his status as a minor celebrity, and he tips the cashier a hundred dollars for her efforts at exchanging his outrageous chip denominations. He strides away with a thick wad of cash in his pockets, smiling through crooked teeth at those less fortunate in their gambling endeavors. *Asshole.*

Sighing, Kalisa steps up to the ATM, and after inserting her card, receives discouraging news from the screen: *There are insufficient funds in your account.*

Bashful at her lowly economic status, Kalisa glances defensively around the area, hoping her money troubles are not too obvious. Unfortunately, several grimacing players notice her precarious financial position, and from their understanding looks, it's a condition they've experienced themselves.

Kalisa clenches her teeth and avoids their stares, almost forgetting to collect her card as she paces toward the exit. Keeping her head down, she concentrates on her feet as she juggles in her mind how she'll replace the funds she's just lost. *Robbing Peter to pay Paul, as usual. What do I do when Peter is broke?*

As Kalisa gets to the casino's main entrance, an imposingly heavy man steps into her path. Looking down with a groveling smile, Ben is ecstatic to see her. Dressed in a security uniform, he speaks in a manner indicating he's developmentally challenged, but his kind face brings a grin to Kalisa's lips.

"Hi, Ben," Kalisa says, and she gives him a hug, or at least tries to extend her arms around his enormous frame in a facsimile of one. "You look handsome as usual. How's work tonight? Did you arrest any bad guys?"

Ben's face blushes red, from the top of his expansive forehead to the bottom of his substantial jowls.

"No, Kalisa. Just a few drunk guys we had to walk out because they were mean," says Ben. "When are you coming back for work? I miss you."

CHAPTER TWO

Kalisa steps back from Ben, looking to either side to make sure nobody else from the security staff has witnessed tonight's epic slot loss.

"I'm on a four-day," Kalisa replies. "I'll be back Tuesday, and we can have some lunch. OK? I need to get home to Seth—I'm late."

Kalisa's smile fades at her own mention of her son. Guilt gnaws at her features as she inclines her head to the door.

Ben takes the hint and steps out of her way. He bends and motions to the door with a flourish, like she's the queen of the casino herself. He raises his eyebrows as their gazes lock, beckoning her on her way in a friendly goodbye.

Kalisa nods self-consciously at the ample-framed man, then rushes out the gleaming glass doors into the descending darkness. Ben watches her go with a pleasant grin.

#

Kalisa drives through the mostly empty streets of Reno in a dilapidated car. Her 1990s sedan pings with an odd sound—several actually—as its engine bemoans its long-serving status as a commuting workhorse. With numerous dents and a color scheme that seems unidentifiable in the fading light, the vehicle screams "it's all I can afford" to the uncaring world around her.

- 21 -

DESPICABLE

Kalisa chews on her lip as she focuses into the scant light provided by her clumsy ride. The headlights throw beams ahead in an off-kilter fashion, like someone rearranged the pattern to fit a driver who is cross-eyed. Kalisa frowns, hoping it will pass inspection the next time it's due. *That's if it makes it that far and doesn't give up the ghost. Why do I always get to drive shitty cars?*

Of course, Kalisa knows the answer to that, but it never hurts to inject a little self-pity into her mood. The truth is that a gambling addiction is expensive, no matter how much she tries to massage the numbers. Car payments are a decidedly difficult endeavor when the running buffaloes of her favorite slot machine are awaiting her insubstantial earnings, and those damn animals never seem to provide a return on her manic investment.

On the dimly lit road outside, she drives past people that have it much worse than her, something that is both comforting and sad. In the gloom of traffic and streetlights, homeless people push carts full of treasured possessions along the sparsely populated streets. Their form of addiction is usually of the substance-abuse kind, but the fact that it's a self-inflicted form of punishment doesn't make the results of crushed hopes and dreams any less tragic.

When Kalisa eases to a stop at a wide intersection in this gritty area of town, her gaze finds an old woman making her way across a crosswalk on a side street. The

CHAPTER TWO

doddering lady half-drags a shopping cart behind her, one that's piled high with her belongings. The clacking wheels of the rusted cart aren't fully cooperating with her movements as she yanks it across the pocked pavement. The image reminds Kalisa of an old cartoon, where some animated character or another is trying to force a sitting horse to get moving by yanking on its reigns.

Frustrated, the woman looks up, panting from the effort and not knowing how to proceed.

Meeting her eyes, Kalisa nods at the woman. The lady's wrinkled face is determined and grimy, and a smudge of deep-red lipstick on her face hearkens back to a time when the wrinkles were absent and the makeup adorned a younger visage. Perhaps she was an attractive woman at some point in the distant past, full of life and bawdy expectations for a yet-unknown future.

Kalisa wonders what makes people end up where they do in life, forcing themselves into such desperate circumstances. Her thoughts are cut short when she realizes her own way through life is beset by similar mistakes of self-sabotage.

Throwing the car in park, Kalisa hurries from the driver's seat and rushes to help the woman. Kalisa quickly drags the clanking cart to the far side of the intersection, making sure it doesn't roll away by jamming it against a hedge. She moves back on the road to help the lady, but she's rewarded with a scowl for her efforts. The unappreciative woman grunts unintelligibly and waves Kalisa away as she stumbles back to her shopping cart.

Left standing in the street with her car idling, Kalisa sighs with reservation. She moves her gaze up and down the thoroughfare, as if someone else will pop out of the darkness to applaud her good-Samaritan behavior. She's always heard it said that the best way to improve your emotional health is to help others, so this was a good start; the problem is, that isn't going to make five hundred bucks reappear in her bank account from tonight's losing escapades.

But all turnarounds begin somewhere, making life a little better—even if for only a few moments. Her son needs her to have a normal life, to guide him through the troubles he will face. That's her job, and it's the most important one she'll ever have. Not many degenerate gamblers make very good mothers.

Suddenly remembering her need to get home, Kalisa emerges from her mental funk and hurries back to the car. As she pulls down the deserted street, the homeless woman doesn't offer her even a second glance.

#

The sidewalk and parking spaces in front of the large apartment complex are as worn down as Kalisa's car. The surrounding tenements are downtrodden, evoking a harsh backdrop filled with the distant booms of bass among poorly backlit structures. Cracks run through the aging asphalt, showing sprouts of weeds working their way up to be a permanent presence amongst numerous beaten-up automobiles.

The buildings of the complex are likewise tawdry in their appearance, with flaking paint and old shingles showcasing them as being one step below the working class. Ramshackle and poor, few of the residents here aspire to a life of wealth and ostentation. Most would settle for comfortable and safe.

Worse, a group of male teens hangs out in the common area of the apartment amongst some benches. Most light bulbs illuminating the pathways that connect the varied buildings aren't functional, but enough light is present to mark the area as potentially menacing for the average person.

Kalisa eases her vehicle into a parking space directly in front of a sign that reads *Carmona Acres*. The decades-old writing is on a weathered image of a beautiful beach. It's difficult to see how these apartments could ever have been part of a beach environment, but that long-ago marketing decision seems to have remained intact. To add to the disused motif of the surrounding area, some enterprising resident has used spray paint to transform the text on the sign to the name of *Carnal Acres*, with the added benefit of painted genitalia for those who may be unfamiliar with the written word.

Grasping her purse and exiting her car, Kalisa moves with the hurried gait of someone who is late. She paces ahead and makes for the gaggle of teens that stand at a central point of the common area—and on the way to her apartment.

Watching her approach, the young men glance at each other, as if deciding who will be the one best-suited to harass Kalisa.

Eddie takes the reigns of the challenge and steps in Kalisa's way. He is a year below legal age and wears a stained wife-beater. He is also stoned, with the blurry look of someone who is just able to interact with his surroundings in a lucid manner.

"Hello, Officer. How ya doing?" asks Eddie, and he lazily moves close to Kalisa, puffing out his sunken-chest to impress his comrades. "Can I help ya with somethin'?"

Kalisa pulls up short of the teen and moves her gaze to his friends, gauging the level of potential hazard from the group. She speaks in a very cool tone, like she's ordering a sandwich—without asking for anything special on it. She has the glimmer of a warning in her eyes for the young man, one that he misses in his degraded state.

"You can get out of my way, Eddie. My son is waiting for me."

Eddie takes a moment to collect himself, then steps closer to Kalisa, where his few inches of extra height allow him to look down on her. He intends for the effect

CHAPTER TWO

to be intimidating, but intimidation is not what's evident in Kalisa's eyes.

"Oh, OK. Anything else I can help ya with?" Eddie asks, and he leers as he inches closer. "You'd be my kinda...old lady."

Kalisa breathes deep and calms herself, though she doesn't appear outwardly bothered. Running through the options for her near future, she decides on a course that will bring her most quickly to her apartment and son.

"Eddie, if you don't get out of my way," says Kalisa, her tone rising as she looks at each of the surrounding boys. "I'm going to ram my knee through your chest...and then make a citizen's arrest on your broken body."

Kalisa points to a ground-level apartment in a nearby building.

"Followed by telling your mother I had to seriously injure you for keeping me from Seth."

After Kalisa's threat, anger flashes in Eddie's eyes...followed by worry. Trying to keep his courage and impress his friends, he remains locked in place, still blocking Kalisa's way forward.

Now, Kalisa leans forward, lowering her voice so that only Eddie can hear.

"Are those things...things that you want to go through, Eddie?" Kalisa asks. "There are better ways to spend your evening."

- 27 -

DESPICABLE

Eddie arches his head back, as if her words alone moved him to dodge. Considering the idea of having his ass kicked by a woman, and then his mom doing more of the same, he makes the easy choice: surrendering and saving face.

Eddie steps to the side and motions graciously ahead, while meeting the gazes of his friends with fake humor.

"Sorry, Officer, just tryin' to be friendly."

Nodding her head, Kalisa walks through the group of now less-confident teens. Each boy avoids glancing at Kalisa as they try to downplay their cowardice in the face of someone who has called their bluff.

Without a look back, Kalisa bounds up several steps at a time on the way to her second-floor apartment.

#

Kalisa gazes down in the dim glow of her son's bedroom. A faint light from a dimmed lamp illuminates the confines of a typical young man's living space, with creature action figures on a desk and posters of monsters providing scary images in the deficient light. A particularly vivid photo of Kurt Russel stares down from a print on one wall, with several horrid beasts from *The Thing* filling in the image around the actor's much-younger face.

Reaching down, Kalisa strokes the hair of her twelve-year-old son Seth. He is peacefully snoozing amidst his

CHAPTER TWO

rumpled covers, wrapped up like a contorted burrito. His complexion is less dark than his mother's, indicating a mixed racial heritage, but his facial features are otherwise a mirror image of Kalisa.

Kalisa continues her stare for several moments before sighing and turning to a lit hallway. She exits his room and emerges into a cozy living room, one that has walls full of colorful kids' paintings and polyester furniture. A worried teen girl, Claire, sits on the couch with a concerned stare. With glasses and an acne problem, she is naturally shy, but there is something else about the impending conversation that's making her uncomfortable.

Trying to put a smile on her guilty features, Kalisa moves to the kitchen to pour a glass of juice.

"How was he tonight?" asks Kalisa, and she tops off the glass. "Any problems?"

"Mrs. Kinigi, everything was great, we played some video games—he always likes the scary ones—and ate pizza."

"He has an active imagination," says Kalisa, letting her pride for Seth seep into her voice. "I appreciate you looking after him while I visited some friends."

The room goes quiet, and Claire studiously avoids making eye contact with Kalisa. She clenches her hands together, massaging her knuckles in an agitated gesture. The lack of conversation is not lost on Kalisa, and she dreads what's coming next.

"Mrs. Kinigi, I need to get home. You said you would be here two hours ago," Claire says.

Trying to hide the abject shame that creeps across her expression, Kalisa walks to the living room and sets the glass of juice in front of the teenager. She looks down and tries to appear confident. Of what, she has no idea, but she learned a long time ago to appear sure of yourself, even when you're holding a losing hand.

"I know, Claire, and I'm sorry. I tried to make it—,"

"You were late last time, too," interrupts Claire, still avoiding looking up. "Can't you let me know when you're gonna be late? My parents get mad at me."

Kalisa looks at the ceiling, breathing deep and trying to sound motherly. She fails miserably, and her voice croaks like a defensive eight-year-old who got caught stealing candy.

"I…know. I'll take you home now," says Kalisa, and she grabs her purse from the kitchen counter, digging out her keys with hurried hands.

Claire shakes her head, then inclines it towards the front door.

"My dad's on his way. He said he wants to talk to you," Claire says, nervously taking a sip from the glass.

"I…understand," replies Kalisa, and she sets down her purse with a resigned grimace.

Holding out a tentative hand, Claire finally ventures a glance toward Kalisa. Her tone is hopeful.

CHAPTER TWO

"Can I get my pay? You said last time you'd pay me double when you didn't have any cash on you."

It's Kalisa's turn to avoid meeting Claire's gaze, and her voice lowers to almost a whisper. Being ashamed is bad enough, but not being able to pay a teen for their labor must make her the worst person in the world.

"I'm sorry, I'm a little short again," Kalisa says, pursing her lips and damning the gambling Gods in her distressed thoughts. "Can you wait until Wednesday? I get paid…"

Claire lowers her hand, disappointed as Kalisa's voice trails off. Several moments of silence intrude, with only the faint hum of the refrigerator to occupy the uncomfortable discussion.

From the front door comes a sharp knock, the knock of someone who is keen to speak with whoever is inside. Kalisa stares at the door, and for a moment she thinks about how strange it is that so much information can be conveyed by such a simple gesture as a firm rap on the wooden door. A timid tap might mean a new salesman or perhaps a person embarking on a first date with a prospective love interest. An intrusive knock could be anything from a jealous lover to a visit by investigating police. This incoming bang is decidedly of the second variety.

"That must be my dad," says Claire, and she stands, relieved and concerned at whatever will happen next.

DESPICABLE

Kalisa frowns worriedly at the young woman. Nodding, she paces to the front door, pasting a fake smile on her face as she prepares to meet Claire's father.

Chapter Three

The receptionist area is clean and proper, with subdued lights illuminating a relaxing collection of chairs in the waiting area. Lining the space around are several framed prints of famous paintings spaced on a fake beige rock wall. Next to a wall-mounted fish tank in the corner is an ornamental trickling fountain, with the whole scene showcasing an expensive designer's efforts to create a calming atmosphere for visitors.

In the middle of the quiet area is a receptionist desk, where a prim woman in her twenties sits and clacks at a keyboard. She peaks down behind her shiny desk, her face locked in a perma-smile, even as she focuses solely on her computer monitor.

Clean wood-paneling above her desk showcases a cool-looking graphical sign, and it offers a bit of wisdom for patients in the form of its flowing calligraphy lettering: *Make Real What Makes You Happy.*

Kalisa sits alone in the corner of the waiting area, trying not to be annoyed at waiting. Glancing at her cheap

DESPICABLE

dial watch, the kind that tries to look expensive but is always priced at less than ten dollars, she sighs out loud and scans the empty waiting area.

The receptionist may have noticed Kalisa's impatience, but she doesn't let it show as she continues with the novel-writing tapping on her unseen screen.

Standing, Kalisa paces in front of the lady and focuses on her with a firm expression. As she tries to get her attention, Kalisa offers a polite tone. The effect is a bit disingenuous, because her face is flushed and obviously unhappy.

"Miss, when will the doctor be able to see me?" asks Kalisa, inclining her head down a short hallway behind the receptionist. "I don't have much time for this today. I got…things to do."

The receptionist mechanically moves her gaze to a clock on the wall, noting the time is five minutes to three PM. She doesn't remind Kalisa her appointment is still a few minutes off, but her patronizing stare indicates she doesn't need to. She does manage to keep a false smile as she meets eyes with Kalisa, which is something of a victory for good manners.

"Dr. Bergstrom will be with you…shortly," says the young receptionist, dropping her scanning eyes back to the monitor.

Kalisa bites back an urge to yell at the woman. Collecting herself, she visibly controls the inclination to confront the arrogant twit. Pondering the moment,

CHAPTER THREE

Kalisa wonders why some workers will who use any power they have to needle those they are supposed to be helping. Such uncaring interaction is a tried and true aspect of worker-customer interaction worldwide, but you'd think it wouldn't be so common in a trauma psychologist's office.

Breathing deep, Kalisa leans forward, clutching the end of the desk and lowering her voice.

"Listen, you glorified—."

The door at the end of the hallway swings open, and Dr, Bergstrom strides out. He is a middle-aged fellow with a face scarred by pockmarks and time. Though a bit stooped-over, he strides with the effusive gait of someone who is used to walking and vigorous exercise. With a concerned glance, he notices the developing conflict between his worker and Kalisa, but his sincere smile melts away all the room's negative emotions—especially Kalisa's.

"So glad you were able to make it, Kalisa." Says Bergstrom, and he drops the corner of his mouth in mild disapproval at the receptionist. "I am at your disposal, completely. Let's get to work in my office."

Shooting a gaze between the two, Kalisa offers a slight grin to the doctor. When Bergstrom gestures backward and turns to his office, Kalisa suppresses the urge to flip off the secretary as she follows behind.

#

Bergstrom's office is clean and presentable, and his furniture is covered with comforting knickknacks to present the area as a cozy place of retreat. On his desk are a ceramic bust of Buddha, spaced between hand-painted figurines of buffaloes and ducks. A miniature farmhouse that must have taken considerable time and money to craft rounds out the relaxation-inducing ensemble.

On one wall is a gorgeous photo of Niagara Falls with its swirling, misty air, while on another, herds of gazelles are stretched across the gorgeous plains of Africa's Serengeti.

Kalisa stops in the middle of the room, focusing on the photos. They have a certain attractiveness to them, but they don't seem to be taken by a professional photographer, making them even more appealing to her untrained eye because of their unrefined quality.

Bergstrom notices her attention.

"I was able to travel around a bit when I was younger," Bergstrom says, and his voice has a unique, monotone quality that manages to be both insightful and unobtrusive. "Between various bouts of study and training, I found the world a most wonderful place to learn about this life that we are all stumbling through."

Kalisa nods but doesn't reply immediately. Looking around, she finds a comfortable couch to sit on and takes a moment to get relaxed. The dark cloth cushions seem to have been made for her personal comfort, and she exhales contentedly as she leans back.

CHAPTER THREE

"You one of those people that sees the world as your oyster? You travel around taking in the sights and think your bucket-list means you're a man of culture?" Kalisa asks, and she is perhaps more judgmental than she intended to be.

Bergstrom takes the dig in stride, and he grins as he finds his place in a leather chair opposite Kalisa.

"Ahh, the life of a young man spending his parent's money to party, while studying, you mean?" Bergstrom counters, managing to sound both unruffled and unoffensive at the same time. "No, I worked my way through school doing odd jobs and attending the cheapest schools in my specialty. My parents were killed in a car accident when I was young, and being a foster kid didn't allow for an extensive inheritance to draw from. My childhood trauma is a big reason I chose this line of work."

Bergstrom points to his credentials in a frame on the wall, and Kalisa notices they have sticky notes with smiley faces attached to them for comedic effect. *Ternopil National Medical University of Ukraine* headlines his medical degree. Kalisa nods and is impressed, understanding that isn't a path to riches often seen in the medical community.

Kalisa looks down at her hands, where she nervously tugs on a jade-jeweled wedding ring. The office is quiet while both consider her circumstances.

DESPICABLE

After the silence continues for several moments, Bergstrom breaks the ice, nodding towards Kalisa. Empathy drips from his words as he speaks in a soft tone.

"The idea is that we have to talk…extensively…about what happened. These kinds of traumas almost never resolve themselves on their own," Bergstrom says, pausing. "No matter how much time passes."

When Kalisa stays quiet and focuses down on her fidgety hands, Bergstrom continues.

"When I was doing my training in Europe, I met a very old man who had been an infantry soldier in the German army during the Second World War. This man had marched from one end of the continent to the other, in Poland, France, Ukraine—on and on. He witnessed death and killing on a scale and ferocity we would find unbelievable in our current times."

Bergstrom stops, his mind focusing back across two decades. His pause makes Kalisa interested, and she raises her head to concentrate on the doctor and his story.

"Freidrich was his name. He had shrugged off the trauma and death for forty years, but one day his family found him in a vegetative state, or something close to it. He was squeezing a baby toy that had recently been given to one of his grandchildren, clutching it in his fingers and squishing the doll over and over again. He simply sat there, staring at the simple plaything and murmuring to himself. In spite of the intervening years of health and

CHAPTER THREE

raising a family, his military experience finally caught up with him, and he shut down completely."

"Wh…what happened to him?" Kalisa asks.

"Unfortunately, the passage of time alone did not solve his intense psychological wounds," Bergstrom says, a sad grimace coming over his features. "And he lived out his remaining time in a Veteran's home, not able to enjoy his final years. We were able to make some progress, but his pain was too acute to completely reverse—or even live with in a fully functional manner."

Kalisa returns her gaze to her lap and realizes there might be other people in the world, people that actually had it as bad or worse than she did. It might not just be her that has a horrible past, a past that haunts and infects everything she is and does. Pain exists in all forms across all cultures and realizing this makes her feel somewhat hopeful.

After a deep breath, she shrugs.

"So, how do I get past this…thing? You got like a machine to hook me up to? Maybe electric shocks or something?"

Bergstrom chuckles, but Kalisa only seems to be half-joking. In fact, she would probably be more than willing to sign up for daily jolts of the painful current if it meant fixing her life.

"No, that will not be necessary, I think," says Bergstrom, still chuckling, and he scribbles on a notepad balanced on his lap. "We can start with your story, and

DESPICABLE

you can tell it in any shape or form you need to. Leave out what you want, include what you want. The reality is you are your own boss, and your will and insight are what will allow us to make progress here. Think of me as merely a conductor on your personal train, but you control our destination in this…journey."

Kalisa doesn't much like that metaphor, because it seems rather childish, almost patronizing in its slick description of her proposed road to recovery. Still, she pushes away her doubts and realizes it can't hurt to try.

Moving her gaze to the ceiling, Kalisa sighs deeply. She lets her muscles relax and inhales the stale office air into her lungs, trying to prepare herself mentally for what comes next. Her eyes grow distant, and she falls into long-ago memories as she relays her story.

Loud cackles of laughter came from outside the house, and the strange sounds were like someone teetering on the edge of sanity. It barely seemed to be a human voice that made the odd and merry sound, because the owner of the disturbing and shrill laugh carried on with his bizarre chuckle, hardly taking time to suck in air between his raspy breaths.

Between these expressions of indeterminate humor came the pleading of voices. Several different voices, those of friends and neighbors, offered muffled begging in response to that unseen and laughing tormentor beyond the wall.

"Please, we have done you no harm. Spare us, in God's name," begged a middle-aged male voice. "We are not——."

CHAPTER THREE

A THUNK interrupted the voice, followed by the thud of a body hitting the ground. Wails of terrified mourning followed, accompanied by disbelieving shrieks from new victims who were waiting their own turn at hand-delivered execution. Listening to the shocking and merciless event was like having an auditory front row to Hell.

Inside, Kalisa's simple home was spartan but attractive. Skimpy rugs were laid across slotted wooden planks throughout the basic structure, and cloth-covered windows kept too much light from seeping in from the afternoon sun. Simple chairs and a table also occupied space in the dim environment, fulfilling its cozy intent.

Except, the home was no longer very homey. Kalisa lay on the floor, seven years old and dressed in a colorful and pretty dress. She was sprawled on the ground, face-down and with a grievous wound on her bloodied back. The almost-clotted blood seeped into her dress, making the colors less pretty and ruining the pleasant image of what should have been an innocent girl.

Coming fully awake, Kalisa's eyes jerked open. Her pain was intense as she grimaced and tried to grab at the back wound, as if touching the deep machete-caused injury would make it feel better.

Glancing over, Kalisa's terrified eyes came to rest on her dear mother. Her mom lay on her back in the middle of the room, her unseeing eyes staring up and to the side. She looked peaceful in her dead state, and except for the mortal slashes across her abdomen, she could have passed for just taking a relaxing nap.

Tilting her head further to the side, Kalisa's gaze came to rest on her brother's canted and sock-less heel, which was still and bloody in the faint light. Mercifully, the rest of his body was not visible from

DESPICABLE

her vantage point, and Kalisa didn't want to flesh out her vision with an image of the rest of his hacked and mutilated body.

Tears flowed freely down Kalisa's dirty cheeks as she struggled to move. A putrid odor drifted in from the curtained windows, along with a smoky haze from an unseen fire that couldn't have been far away. As she struggled to crawl ahead, she stifled the urge to scream from her physical and emotional pain; to do so would have brought immediate death from the butchering psychopaths standing just beyond her home's walls.

Pursing her lips, Kalisa dragged herself along, focusing on an open closet on the inner wall of the house. As she scooted ahead, her eyes concentrated manically with each squirming lunge toward the closet. Each painful move toward it became her sole focus in the whole world—nothing else mattered. She allowed nothing to intrude on her thoughts, and even her dead family was forced from her mind as she approached a thick rug on that closet floor.

Reaching into the dark space, Kalisa's bloodied fingers found the end of old rug in the enclosed area. Using what little strength she had, she pulled it aside and gently lifted a trap door in the confined area.

Kalisa's terror-stricken eyes bulged from the effort of pulling herself into the trap door. Dropping down, she lowered herself into a dank hiding space in the lightless area. She allowed neither a moan nor a scraping sound to accompany her descent into the tight interior of the dusty spot.

Using her final energy, Kalisa was able to reach up and lower the trap door, and she tugged the corner of the rug to hide her passage into that momentary place of safety.

CHAPTER THREE

Gasping from the effort, Kalisa leaned on her side, struggling for air and curling into a fetal position. Exhausted and overwhelmed, she drifted off.

#

Later, Kalisa awoke to silence and night shadows above her. Peering up through slots in the floorboards, she was able to make out light entering her home from flame and moonlight filtering through the home's exterior windows. This eerie backlight made the area above even creepier and more mysterious in its solitude, like Kalisa was suddenly the last person alive in this town; in fact, after what recently happened, that might well have been the case.

The sounds of desperation and slaughter from outside had stopped, and only the distant crackle of flames drew Kalisa's wary attention into the early night. If not for mass killings, it would have seemed a normal occasion in the community, one filled with customary interaction and neighborly affection. But now, only the faint licking of fire and unnatural silence were evident to the cowering young girl.

After some moments of quiet, a new sound came from inside the home: a scraping, like a movement of a dead weight across the floor above Kalisa. Holding her breath to remain quiet, Kalisa waited and watched with terrified anticipation. As she grimaced from the pain of her wound, she focused up and across the dusty floor, searching with hope for the source of the new sound.

DESPICABLE

At the corner of their living room, Kalisa caught the barely visible shadow of a figure being dragged from the home. It was the body of her mother, unmoving and uncaring in its permanent state, being quietly yanked toward the doorway.

Someone had come to take her mom from this cursed place. It could be a relative or friend if any had survived, but something about the dark figure pulling on the corpse flashed a warning in Kalisa's mind. As if momentarily waking from her recent death, Kalisa heard her mom's faint whisper in her petrified mind: "Stay hidden, daughter; the nightmare is not yet over."

More time passed, and that shadowy form returned to retrieve her brother's body. Pulling his limp weight across the floor, a path of her brother's blood left a dragging mark as the stranger tugged his corpse across the wooden boards. Revoltingly, his blood continued to leak from his unseen wounds, dripping down through spaces in the wooden planks. The rivulets of his life force collected under the floor in streaks as he was also moved from the house into the vague light outside.

Overwhelmed at the enormity of the carnage and having her place in the world so thoroughly destroyed, Kalisa began to hyperventilate. Breathing faster and faster, she gasped as she tried to control her breathing. Her fear of being discovered accelerated, and each passing moment brought more and louder sucking of air. As she lost her battle for silence, it was as if all the oxygen in the world was unable to fill her desperate lungs. Her chest labored as she struggled to find enough life-giving air in the confines of the dim crawlspace.

CHAPTER THREE

From outside, the shadowy form seemed to notice. Letting Kalisa's brother flop to the ground, the figure turned back toward her house. A loud sniffing sound accompanied his head movements as he focused on the door. He crept ahead, moving again to reenter the home.

Kalisa could hear the sniffing as the stranger stood in the night. She realized her hope for safety had evaporated and leaned back in the darkness, accepting her fate. Shaking away her struggles for breath, she determined not to scream when the end came; at least she would be with her mom and brother again soon. Death is not such a bad thing when it brings immediate reunion with loved ones, even for the uninformed mind of a child.

It was a peaceful thought as the stranger stopped at the doorway, and Kalisa could see that his shadowed form was large, barely able to fit through the diminutive opening. The unseen face focused across the room to her closet floor, and Kalisa could almost feel a grin forming on the hidden facial features of the stranger.

A flash of firelight shone off an abruptly emerging machete, swung from the darkness behind the stranger. With a sickening wet-fruit sound, the stranger's head was brutally cleaved in half, and Kalisa's pursuer collapsed in a heap to the side of the suddenly empty doorway.

Confused, Kalisa's eyes flitted around, looking for her savior— or perhaps a new aggressor. Not knowing why or what exactly happened, Kalisa concentrated on the doorway again. Her fear had somehow dissipated, and she arched her back and stretched her neck to get a better view through the planks of the floor.

DESPICABLE

A new man strode into the house, stopping in the middle of the room. He was also tall and well built, looking a bit like a svelte lumberjack in the subdued light. In one hand he wielded his machete, and it now dripped with blood. As drops of the dark liquid mixed with the collected gore of her mom and brother on the ground, the man focused toward her. He looked directly at Kalisa, seemingly fully aware of her presence. As rays of light partially illuminated his shadowed face, a smile formed on the outlines of his amused lips.

The room is quiet as Kalisa emerges from her thoughts and memories. Her dark brow is sweat-covered in the cool office, and she works her lips as she nervously tries to chew on her cheek.

Flustered, Kalisa raises her gaze to the ceiling in a silent prayer to the God she hopes is listening: *Please let me forget. I don't want to remember this anymore.*

For just a second it felt like she was there, living amongst those long-dead ghosts of her demonic past experiences. Kalisa lowers her eyes, wondering why the great memories of her life, like the birth of her child or falling in love for the first time, cannot be similarly re-experienced.

Bergstrom stares at her from his chair, his face the picture of empathy. His eyes don't waver as he takes in Kalisa's movements and raw emotions, vacuuming up her distress with his professional and caring demeanor.

"That…is truly horrible, one of the worst things I've ever heard," Bergstrom says, and he somehow manages

CHAPTER THREE

to sound like he's her best friend as he leans closer. "For a child to see such things makes life's normal...troubles seem quaint in comparison."

The room is silent for a time as Bergstrom waits for some input from Kalisa. The wait is long, but Kalisa manages to sound controlled when she finally speaks again.

"The guy with the machete saved my life," says Kalisa, her expression growing distant at the memory of being saved. "I don't know who he was, but he left, even though I know he knew I was there."

Kalisa looks down at her hands, where she curls and flexes them as she ponders those distant events. Noticeably, there are numerous white scars on her knuckles. Bergstrom takes notice of the old injuries and waits again for more words from the despondent Kalisa.

"Two days later I was found by a Hutu neighbor," Kalisa says. "She hid me in her basement until the crowds of roving maniacs left our town. That was it, the end of the genocide—at least where I was."

Nodding, Bergstrom stands and moves to a wall of shiny books that probably have never been read, at least here. As he peers at the spines of thick medical tomes, he offers a distant look of his own, and his tone becomes contemplative.

"Even in times of great evil, Kalisa, people were willing to risk everything, including their own lives, to help you. Perhaps that's something worth remembering?

- 47 -

DESPICABLE

There is always a silver lining to our experiences in life, even when they seem paltry in comparison."

Kalisa considers that thought, running over how many silver linings she's managed to accrue in her life. Not enough for a silver dollar, she reckons, and she cringes at the thought of gauging success by luck or positive thinking.

Standing, Kalisa moves to the window and gazes out, where she fixates on a cat that's making its way across a busy street. The wary animal is trying to avoid getting squished as it gets to where it has to be. It's an image she understands in a very poignant way.

Turning back to Bergstrom, she tries to avoid sounding like a bitch as meets his eyes.

"True, Doc, but there were way more evil assholes there than good people. Way more, so it doesn't make me feel all that hopeful."

Bergstrom nods and lowers his voice, affecting that friendly vibe that could charm a wolf away from a recent kill. Or several wolves.

"I understand. I'm here to help. It's important as we work through your trauma that you understand, you are not alone. You've taken the first step to recovery, and that's always the most difficult part. You'd be surprised how many people are unable to do even that."

"I finally got good insurance," replies Kalisa, and the glimmer of a smile crosses her features. Something like hope bubbles under her hard-edged skepticism, and for a moment she allows herself to feel optimistic about her future.

#

The night is drizzly, and light filters through a puffy mist in the robust parking area. The lot is full of recreational vehicles, cars, and SUVs, and they are arranged haphazardly in enormous open spaces stretching into the darkness. Several rows of humming streetlights illuminate portions of public parking, making the twenty-story casino at its center appear like a nerve center to its rows of gambling visitors.

Most of the places for parking are filled with regular working-class vehicles, but the closer to the main entrance of the neon-lit casino, the more they are of the luxury variety. The casino's VIP clientele get to park closer to the entrance due to their higher gaming contributions, with placards of "VIP gold club" or "Platinum" announcing a certain amount of privilege to the establishment's customers.

Kalisa stands not far from the main entrance to the casino, where its clean-windowed doors are just visible at the dark periphery of her vision. She's wearing a security uniform and has a confused look as she stares up at the patterns of a large glowing sign that advertises "Pai-Gow Progressive Bonus 153,254 Reno's LARGEST."

DESPICABLE

To her side stands her colleague, Darryl. He is similarly attired in a cheap uniform, but his too-big shirt hangs loosely over his slight frame. While Kalisa is fit and attractive, Darryl looks like he skipped one-too-many meals in his middle-aged life. Completing the unkempt appearance, his scruffy red and gray stubble looks to have missed a shave.

Still, his enthusiastic eyes are alive and happy as he exchanges pleasant glances with Kalisa.

"I can't imagine what the electricity bills alone must be," muses Kalisa, and she pans her head to take in each of several lighted advertisements that cover the imposing block building.

Darryl grins as he follows Kalisa's gaze around the exterior of the casino. Hesitating, he stops himself from speaking when a destitute player ambles by on the way home to lick his gambling wounds. Darryl frowns and takes the time to nod to the sad and disheveled fellow in a show of blue-collar solidarity.

Readjusting his gaze, Darryl snorts, nodding up at the casino's gaudy sign on the top of its highest floor, *Grand Parkway Gaming and Sportsbook*.

"If they revealed that, all the gamblers would stop making their bets, and might actually save some money. My cousin says he puts a hundred bucks in his bank account every time he gets invited to gamble, then stays home when it's time to go. Says he's got thousands in an account now, savin' it for a rainy day."

CHAPTER THREE

Kalisa's lively smile fades at that personal anecdote, and she imagines she might own half of rural Nevada if she had taken that same path over the last fifteen years. It's funny how good choices compound with interest over time, while shitty ones tend to leave their catastrophic imprints on your life immediately.

"I doubt it, Darryl. They get half my income back, even after paying me garbage. Us gambling degenerates never seem to learn."

Darryl thinks on that, then cocks his head toward the gambling mothership. Even from out here, a crowd of shouting players can be heard inside, crowing over some fleeting gaming victory.

"Half of Reno is in hock to the casinos. You ain't the only one chasing wealth on bad odds," says Darryl, and his face cracks into an empathetic grin.

Before Kalisa can thank him for his understanding, a radio at her waist chirps with a female dispatcher's uninterested drawl. It's the voice of someone who's not exactly happy with her career choice.

"Hey Kalisa, we got a report of some drunk guy acting nuts in the South Lot. Can you guys check it out?"

Pulling out her flashlight, Kalisa clicks its button, checking the beam several times. She nods to Darryl and points to the darkness that covers the back of the casino, the part facing away from crowds and traffic. As they pace towards the far side of the cavernous central building of the casino complex, she speaks into her radio.

"On the way."

#

A white stretch limousine is slatted across several parking spaces, taking up too much space—like its driver intended to annoy as many other customers as possible. The area around the enormous limo contains a mishmash of parked buses, trucks, and cars, all of which are empty and quiet.

The dimly lit confines of the nearby environment are dark, almost as if the casino made a calculated effort to lower their electricity bills by ignoring this out-of-the-way portion of the outer parking lot.

Matching the isolated motif, no pedestrians walk through the vague light of the jumbled parking spaces. Most of the vehicles are here for long-term stays, and their owners would rarely venture out to check their vehicles, particularly in the late night. It's a perfect location for some privacy away from the boisterous and crowded casino.

A pudgy man sticks his head out of the limo's long sunroof. Righting himself, the man raises his voice to sing into the dark and remote corner of the paved lot. He wears a ruffled tuxedo, and his face is flushed and sweaty. Amusingly, a white garter belt is affixed around his head, giving him the appearance of a drunken commando.

CHAPTER THREE

His droopy and intoxicated eyes are unfocused as he belts out the words to baseball's S*eventh Inning Stretch*. "Take me out to the ball game...take me out to the park...buy me some peanuts...with...cracker jacks....eh."

Forgetting or perhaps not knowing the rest of the words, the man holds up a bottle of champagne and takes a long pull of the sparkling wine. After finishing the container, he shakes it to determine if there's any more liquid goodness left inside. His exaggerated blinking eyes concentrate on the booze bottle, willing it to provide him more.

With no more spirits to be had from the now-empty bottle, the frustrated man heaves it away, where it shatters on the back bumper of a nearby Range Rover. Giving up on finding the words to his music, he falls into a hum as he focuses up into the night. He pumps his arms high into the air as he grooves to the beat of a song only heard in his own head.

From fifty yards away, another perspective focuses on the drunken reveler. Through a view that's a luminescent and pale green light, the unseen creature watches quietly. The face of the tuxedo man is a darker green from his body heat, while a backlight of residual energy from the day also leaves some glow on the vehicles all around him. The effect is something like night-vision goggles, but it's also sharper, like that of an attentive predator.

Creeping closer, the view of the man gets sharper still, and the creature concentrates fully on the man's face, sizing up the prospective prey. As it gets near, humming from the man's throat is loud and enticing to the superior hearing of the creature. It focuses on the jowls of the man's neck, and it hears the thump of his pulse and the rush of his blood behind the throaty drone of his unintelligible tune.

From far to the side, Kalisa and Darryl interrupt the creature's stalking. Pacing across the parking lot from the dark side of the casino, Kalisa's flashlight shines a green illuminating beam in front of her as it sweeps towards the limousine and its occupant. The incoming security guards' faces and exposed limbs are also visible in the light of the creature's peculiar vision.

Walking close to the limo, Kalisa shines her light on the man and notes the garter belt around his head. Stifling a grin, she addresses him with a fake-respectful tone, one that's universally employed by police and security. "Sir, how are you tonight? Are you staying at the hotel?"

The drunk's lazy gaze moves down to Kalisa. "They all left me here…just because I wanted to partee…more."

"That happens, sir," responds Kalisa, and she glances to Darryl, who watches the spectacle with an ear-to-ear grin. "Why don't you come out of the car? We can talk about it and get you pointed in the right direction of your friends."

"I would," says the man, and he tries to pull himself up through the sunroof. His chubby frame and lack of agility prevent the maneuver. "But I'm stuck…here."

Kalisa motions down to the vehicle's tinted-window doors. "Just come down through one of the doors, sir. We don't want you to fall off the roof."

CHAPTER THREE

The drunken man ponders Kalisa's words, then nods and grins, as if she's divulged the secret to eternal life. He lowers himself, shuffling around inside the car. After several moments of internal banging and frustrated gasps of exertion, one of the windows lowers.

His forlorn face peeks from inside.

"The locks don't work," the man says, and with great effort he leans out the window, squeezing his body through to escape the limo's half-open window.

Unexpectedly, the man vomits a great gout of puke on the white exterior of the luxury vehicle. Several more elongated retches leave the door and area covered with chunky bile. The labors of his post-puke breathing fill the silence as the inebriated man stares down at his steaming vomit.

"I don't feel…right," he says, and he now appears completely stuck when tries to pull himself back inside the vehicle.

Wrinkling her nose, Kalisa gazes over to Darryl, whose expression grows even more amused.

"Must've been quite a party," exclaims Darryl, and his earnest chuckles force a smile to Kalisa's lips. She shakes her head at the gross but entertaining sight.

From behind, a sudden scraping sound comes from in the back of one of the vehicles. Kalisa and Darryl spin around, their expressions suddenly serious. Watching the cone of light from Kalisa's flashlight, they search for the source of the sound.

Nothing is there; the area is empty.

Raising an eyebrow, Kalisa motions to Darryl, and they step gingerly between a row of cars. Kalisa is in the lead, while Darryl follows closely behind, his hand on his baton. Being unarmed, they aren't exactly Starsky and Hutch, but Kalisa's hand hovers near her own baton as she pans her beam around the dark surroundings.

The creature watches from several cars away, its eyes focusing on Kalisa. As they get closer, it lowers itself, keeping out of view. When they've advanced to within a few yards, the creature darts behind another row of vehicles, moving quietly away.

With frightening speed, the creature lunges past the advancing duo, circling behind them as they advance on its former hiding spot. Neither Kalisa nor Darryl notice its passing as they peer suspiciously ahead.

Now it's behind them both. It creeps closer to the unsuspecting guards, its eyes concentrated solely on Kalisa. Within a dozen feet, the unseen predator sniffs gently, taking in the scent of its quarry and getting ready to leap.

From the direction of the casino, a hulking figure trudges its way out of the darkness. Ben moves with a ponderous gait as he labors with hurried steps towards his coworkers. He holds up a hand to get their attention.

The creature swivels to evaluate the incoming threat. Its vision concentrates on Ben, seeing that Ben's complexion is a lighter shade of green against the backdrop of the casino lights. The creature stays still, stopping its advance as it awaits the new security threat.

CHAPTER THREE

As Ben gets closer, his gaze moves to where the creature is hidden, but he doesn't appear to notice the aggressor. He looks back to Kalisa and Darryl, raising his voice through rasps of his hard breathing.

"Hi, Kalisa," shouts Ben, his kind voice breaking the calm silence of the parking lot. "The boss told me to come get you."

Abruptly, the creature flees unseen into the night, with only the smallest of sounds in its wake. Ben's head moves again in its direction, then back to his colleagues.

With nothing left to investigate, Kalisa and Darryl face Ben. Kalisa speaks up, her face serious and bothered. "Hi, Ben," says Kalisa, raising her voice in appreciation. "Good to see you. We were just checking out…the area. What does Erin want?"

Ben's never-ending smile widens as he steps close to Kalisa. He nods amicably at Darryl, but it's obvious who he prefers to talk to. "She says only you can watch the money count today. She says only you know how—everyone else is bad at math."

Kalisa breaks into a smile at her tall and wide friend. She puts a hand on his arm and speaks in a soft voice, nodding up at his eager-to-please face. "Okay, I'll go in. Can you help Darryl with Mr. Personality over there?"

Ben agrees with a nod and a glance toward the limo. Just then, the stuck man manages to pull himself back inside. With a thump against the limo floor, he groans, then raises his voice from the dark interior.

"I told him, 'Don't marry her.' Why didn't he listen to me...why doesn't anyone ever listen to me?"

Nodding to Ben and Darryl, Kalisa shakes her head and paces towards the casino.

As she walks away, Darryl chuckles even louder than before. His grin is infectious as he gestures to the puke-covered car. "I friggin' love this job."

Chapter Four

Late-afternoon sunlight bleeds through half-closed curtains, illuminating a faded but serviceable kitchen. Sounds of playing children drift through tattered screens outside the partially open windowpanes, creating an appealing audible atmosphere within the apartment.

Standing at a well-worn sink, Kalisa looks down at the beige Formica countertops, picking at the scarred edges of a surface probably installed during the final years of the Carter Administration.

Sighing, Kalisa raises her eyes and peers out the windows, where the view shows a tawdry playground in the middle of the building complex. Amongst a broken-down swing set and sandboxes with extensive weeds, several children play without worry or hesitation. Smiling faintly, Kalisa realizes that children could care less about how upscale the equipment is, as long as there's fun to be had with friends.

The smile fades from Kalisa's features as she thinks more on that. There was a time in far-off Rwanda when she had all varieties of friends, and she spent her time with them in a similar way, passing those youthful days with games and gossip. Where are those old friends from carefree times now, the ones that told jokes and shared secrets in the fading afternoon light?

Grimacing, she knows the answer. *They're almost all surely dead, left to rot in forgotten ditches by evil people.*

Turning from the window, Kalisa walks to Seth, who sits at a sturdy hand-built table near the kitchen. The boy scrunches his face in frustration over his schoolbooks, looking through some papers that list the ingredients needed to build a mock volcano. He's overwhelmed, and his eyes dart about the paper, trying to manage his school project as he writes.

"Mom, Mrs. Rodriguez said we have to be done by next Friday," says Seth, his voice rising. "I'm never gonna finish it on time."

Kalisa places a calming hand on his shoulder and offers a reassuring squeeze. "Yes, you will, honey. Your dad said he'd work on it with you this whole weekend. You have plenty of time."

Seth's mood turns sour at the mention of his father, and Kalisa's temperament also worsens at her mention of his dad. The room goes quiet, and Kalisa strokes Seth's hair in sad contemplation.

From the counter near a bowl of messy pancake batter, Kalisa's phone begins to buzz from a call. She moves to look at its screen, seeing "dad" on her mobile.

CHAPTER FOUR

She wants to answer, but decides a call back later is a better option to deal with her father.

Turning around and leaning against the counter, Kalisa puts on an enthusiastic face. Sounding excited, she tries to buoy the room's depressing mood. "When you finish today's assignment, we can eat pancakes…then watch a scary movie."

Seth's expression breaks into an infectious grin, and he scribbles faster as he tries to finish his schoolwork. There's nothing like the prospect of entertainment to hurry along dreaded homework to completion.

"But no blood and guts," adds Kalisa, lowering her tone to break the bad news. "No more nightmares for you."

Frowning, Seth writes slower, suddenly less excited.

On the counter, the phone buzzes again with its vibrating intrusion. Kalisa looks at it again, her face becoming worried. She picks it up and answers with a reserved tone.

"Yes, dad?" she says, and her expression becomes crestfallen as she listens. "I…don't…when did it happen?"

Kalisa raises one hand to her cheek in a shocked gesture as the one-sided conversation continues. "Okay…I'll meet you there tomorrow. Give me some time to figure out when's the best time."

Setting the phone aside, Kalisa takes some time to collect herself. As with the rest of her life, good moments of cheer are soon replaced by bad news. She moves behind her son and places her hands on his shoulders.

As Seth continues his assignment, Kalisa looks out the window, her eyes unfocused. Tears well up and she breathes in controlled gasps, processing yet more emotional trauma.

#

Martin Nigimi sits on a weathered bench in the afternoon light. In his early sixties, he is a sad man, and he looks ahead with deep frown lines covering his sullen face. Unmoving, he is perched and contemplative, as if he's a dark statue molded to stoic perfection.

Above, the overcast sky's errant sunlight shines off his horn-rimmed glasses, and its patchy clouds roll by, like they're in a sprint from one horizon to another. Martin raises his eyes to look into the fluffy structures, taking in their outlines with a detached and gloomy grimace.

Around Martin is an extended lawn, one that's meticulously kept and perfectly green. If not for the occasional colored flower to brighten the landscape, the lawn could pass for fake turf—or even the type that's spray-painted over dead yards in areas facing severe droughts.

The surrounding area is also expertly maintained, showing prim hedges and well-tended greenery leading to a large single-story business. The sprawling building is

CHAPTER FOUR

quiet and unassuming, with its reserved and unimposing walls painted dark brown over wooden siding. Set around the structure is a large lot of uncracked pavement, crisscrossed by recently painted parking lines. Several cars sit unattended in the sparsely populated stalls, and a wide paved road arches to the back of the building and some loading docks.

To Martin's side, a sign faces the road, announcing *Baudin's Funeral Home*. The large, clean letters on the placard are etched to perfection, with flowing black calligraphy over a shiny white background.

Kalisa's car exits from the road fronting the large property. Easing her vehicle to the curb near her father, she lowers the window as she meets his stare. For several moments neither says a word, and they peer at each other like suspicious strangers, with no mirth or smiles of greetings.

Pulling his eyes away, Martin motions for Kalisa to pull her car into the lot, and he stands as her vehicle edges into the quiet area. As Kalisa backs the vehicle into a space, Martin frowns at its poor condition and mild screech of a loose belt in its engine.

Emerging from her car, Kalisa meets Martin halfway through the lot. He is taller than her, a man that has had the advantage of considerable height throughout his life, but he's also aged and is growing stooped by the rigors of time.

"Dad, why didn't you tell me sooner?" asks Kalisa, her voice sad and disappointed. "He died two days ago?"

Scowling, Martin leans close to Kalisa. His gravelly tone, spoken with the accent of an English speaker from the African subcontinent, is not that of a happy father. "You couldn't be bothered to visit him when he was alive. What is the hurry now?"

Kalisa recoils from the verbal blow but still manages to take it like a seasoned boxer. She tries to be respectful as she pushes on. "Dad, I loved grandpa. Do you think he would want us to fight…now?"

Martin stares through his glasses with a grave and judgmental glare. Peering down, he looks intense and disapproving, like Malcolm X at his most self-righteous moment. Intimidated, Kalisa peels her eyes away as she considers the wisdom of having come to meet him.

Abruptly, Martin nods and moves toward the main door of the funeral home, not waiting or seemingly caring if Kalisa follows.

Kalisa stares at the ground for a moment in quiet frustration, then collects her thoughts before dutifully plodding after him.

#

The reception area of the funeral home is pleasant and calm. Lights are recessed in regular spaces on the wooden walls, casting a gentle glow across the expensive paneling

CHAPTER FOUR

of the interior. Numerous clean couches and matching chairs are spread throughout the large room, with wooden coffee tables placed at comfortable intervals between. The windows are encased by attractive and sturdy curtains, serving to shield the room from excessive outside light.

Gentle music accompanies the peaceful space, matching the expectations of a place only visited by the general public when death and mourning are the reasons for a visit.

Kalisa holds her face in a somber expression, staring nervously at the far side of the room's interior wall. An entrance to another room is there, and vases of bright flowers guard either side of its double doors.

Martin walks ahead of her, pacing carefully toward the opening. His features are determined and unflinching as he strides into the viewing room.

Following him in, Kalisa peeks ahead to glance at her grandfather, James Kinigi. Lying in contented repose, the aged corpse is a spitting image of her own dad. Reclined in his coffin, his hands are crossed in the customary fashion, and a shiny crucifix is wrapped around his cold fingers. He looks at peace in his final earthly pose, ready for what comes next.

Martin peers down at his father, his face an image of self-control. Only a slight tremble in his jaw reveals his wavering need to mourn, and he sways as he transfers weight from one foot to another. Kalisa notices the struggle for control and averts her eyes, looking again to her grandfather. They stand for several moments of halting silence, each puzzling over their internal thoughts.

It occurs to Kalisa that she is less moved by this death than her father. There seems to be something about seeing death from two generations away that makes it seem acceptable, like it's the way it should be. In contrast, when it is your own parent that has passed, no matter how old either of you is, the mental trauma is felt far harder, almost to the point of eviscerating your soul. *Nobody knows that better than me.*

Kalisa leans down and kisses James on the forehead. The dead and hard flesh isn't pleasant to the touch, but she feels she has to do something to honor him.

Turning to Martin, she talks in a calm voice, as if not wanting anyone else in the empty room to listen. "He looks good. He led a good life."

Martin moves his gaze to Kalisa, but he doesn't speak. His demeanor is cold, as if her saying anything now is inappropriate. Kalisa sighs and looks away at the snub.

From behind, someone clears his throat in a polite interruption. Kalisa pivots to see a tall man standing there, watching the father and daughter. Kalisa is a bit surprised, as she had no sign of him earlier.

Mathias Baudin is tall, black and deep into middle age, but his eyes are vigorous and youthful. He speaks in a practiced and calm voice, and though he has a French accent, his command of English is flawless.

CHAPTER FOUR

"He lived a long and fruitful life," says Baudin, moving his respectful gaze between the duo. "A life lived well, with many friends and few enemies. How many people in our present…world can say they have lived in such a way?"

Perplexed, Kalisa stares at the interloper with some reservation. She looks back to her dad, but Martin has resumed an overwatch of his deceased father.

"Who are you?" asks Kalisa, trying to be polite.

Mathias lowers his head in a slight bow, then indicates the building around them with raised arms. "I am Mathias Baudin, owner of Baudin Funeral Home. I wish to offer my condolences——."

"You can speak normally here. You're not going to wake anyone," says Kalisa.

Mathias considers her words and extends his hand, ignoring Kalisa's curt behavior. She takes it in a shake and is surprised at its firmness and strength.

Continuing to hold his hand, she tilts her head, as if trying to figure something out. When she can't quite find what tickles at her memory, she releases his fingers and looks back to her grandfather.

"He was a good man, but he had to witness a lot of shitty things in his life," Kalisa says.

Martin emerges from his silence, speaking in a strong voice and surprising Kalisa. "Family was always first for him, daughter. He tried to make up for what happened, but he was ignored."

There's silence for a time. Kalisa grinds her jaw, dealing with a litany of emotions—from shame to sorrow, then anger. Breathing deep, she turns to Mathias. "When will the service be?"

"This Sunday," replies Mathias, assuming a professional death-salesman expression. "We will inter his ashes—,"

"Ashes?" Kalisa asks, and her eyes grow sharp and combative. "He's being cremated?"

Mathias doesn't immediately respond, merely looking over to Martin. Chagrined, Martin shakes his head sadly, obviously not happy about the need to cremate his father.

"I was informed that cost was an issue," Mathias continues, allowing an understanding smile to cross his features. "Our most inexpensive burial—,"

"We're not cremating him," interrupts Kalisa, shaking her head. "No matter the cost, not matter what I have to do, he will not be burned."

"Mrs. Nigimi, it's very common today," Mathias responds, "and religious objections are no longer an issue, due to…"

Kalisa claps her hands together, bringing a stop to the debate. She raises her voice, giving up the polite ruse and focusing on Mathias. "He isn't being burned, period—end of discussion," Kalisa says, and she stares at Mathias, challenging him with her eyes.

CHAPTER FOUR

In response, Mathias shrugs innocently. Reluctantly, he meets Kalisa's intense gaze and agrees with a restrained smile.

Chapter Five

Kalisa sighs, her eyes focused on the moonless night. The blooming lights of the familiar casino are behind her, and she wears a pressed and well-fitted security uniform. In spite of her personal troubles, she's always managed to keep fit and look reasonably presentable, even if it's only on duty.

The look on her face says it all about her job, this profession that has her throwing out drunks from the hotel or holding rowdy partiers for the local cops to pick up. She likes her colleagues and the interaction the job brings, but she could never understand why the pay sucks so badly. It's not like this area is cheap to live in, so why does the work offer such poor economic prospects? *There's got to be something better in my future.*

In front of her is an odd site, the only one of its kind in Reno. A small man-made lake lies at the far end of the property, and in the middle of its glassy surface is a tiny island. A flag sticks from that strange piece of land, and on the shore is a driving range for golf enthusiasts to aim their drives from.

Kalisa imagines that many a drunk golfer has spent hours plinking away at the distant target, trying to see how many of their golf balls they can land on the small strip of island. Better yet, she imagines many a drunken betting match has broken out amongst the participants of such golfing practice, trying to see who can land more shots on the lonely plot in the middle of the water. *That's gotta be the only thing that would make it exciting.*

With it being night, both the island and the driving range are lit by luminescent lampposts, and the bland landscape is adequately illuminated under their glowing bulbs. The sky is clear, with clouds and the faint moon producing a pleasant glow—a nice distraction from the mists and fogginess that often intrude on the area. Kalisa takes a deep breath, appreciating the fresh and clean air.

One lonely golfer stands in the driving range. A middle-aged man of substantial girth, he takes his time as he swigs from a beer bottle. Setting the drink aside, he spends an extended period lining up his shot, until it seems that his preparatory movements with his club will put Kalisa to sleep long before he ever strikes the ball. Kalisa unintentionally holds her breath as she waits for him to hit the damn thing.

Finally, the pudgy man drives the golf ball with a grunt, and it arcs badly to the left of his island target. With a disappointed shake of his head, the man returns to his

CHAPTER FIVE

bottle, taking a long drink as contemplates his next attempt.

With dulled senses, the man finally notices Kalisa's attention, and he waves her way in a friendly gesture. Kalisa returns the acknowledgment with her own wave and grins at the interaction, however brief. The thing about this job is you are often starved for personal contact, at least the type you actually want. Kalisa imagines if she got an office job, regular human contact would be common, but she also knows she would lose her mind if she had to tap at a keyboard more than five minutes per day.

Sighing again, Kalisa turns and paces toward a golf cart parked a few yards away. The cart is the type present at every country club, where old men drive around courses chasing white balls in pursuit of golfing infamy. On this vehicle, there's a cheap sticker with "Security" denoting its purpose.

Kalisa hops into the cart and pulls away with a whir of its electric engine. As she accelerates, her gaze roams the exterior of the lake, looking for something to take her mind off the tedium of the job.

From a deep culvert some distance away, the *creature watches Kalisa. Its green-tinged vision focuses on her, and its acute senses take in each turn of her head and gulp of her throat. Peering at her, the unseen creature is just able to hear the distant thump of her heart.*

Its manic attention on her is absolute, and its pulse quickens with each expectant examination of her movements. For her entire route around the small lake, the creature is only interested in Kalisa, like she's the sole reason for its primal existence.

Finishing her rounds on the small cart, Kalisa aims it back towards the casino. As her vision moves to the distant lights of her base, the creature emerges from its hiding place. Creeping from the shadow of the drainage area, its vision moves to the back of Kalisa. She's unaware of its presence.

But the creature's focus changes. It shifts its vision to the golfer, who is just completing his next shot, one that also misses wide of the mark. His face and jowls are dark green, showing his blood-engorged features in the crisp night air.

"Fuck," shouts the man.

Frustrated, the golfer stands back and picks up another ball. Setting it on a tee, he makes a great show of preparing himself for the next shot, like it's the final attempt for the win at some lofty PGA championship. With an "oomph" he sends the ball on its way, watching it sail through the night sky. As it falls, his excited eyes follow its descent.

The ball lands in the middle of the island, coming to a stop directly next to the flag. It's a perfect shot, and the rotund golfer pumps his arm in victory. He follows with an exuberant dance of celebration, enjoying his triumph like an enthusiastic boy.

CHAPTER FIVE

The golfer turns about to see if anyone else has witnessed his master shot, but his grin falters. His face can't quite comprehend what's coming his way, and his eyes bulge in terror as the creature closes on him.

"Aiiiahhhhhh," comes the scream from the golfer.

Kalisa jerks her head around, stopping the cart from its return trip to the casino. Her features grow confused as she gets off the vehicle. Producing her flashlight, she pans it about, scanning the perimeter of the lake for the source of the sound.

Kalisa understands that sound of pain and terror, the same she heard many times in her distant past. Pacing back to the driving range, she moves her light over the area where the golfer stood just moments before. Perplexed, she stabs the beam into the darkness, searching for the source of the anguished scream. Her worried eyes probe every inch of the driving range, and her hand drops protectively to the handle of her baton.

Nothing. Nobody is here. Walking to where the golfer had been, Kalisa crouches where he just stood. His golf club lies there, and it looks like an expensive one. *What the fuck?*

Kalisa keys her radio, grimacing as she talks. "Dispatch, something just happened out here. Someone is missing from the driving range and…I heard a scream. Call RPD, tell them to hurry. I'm gonna have a look around."

DESPICABLE

"Copy, Kalisa," says the dispatcher, her voice clearly worried. "Be careful; I'm sending everyone to your location."

Standing, Kalisa walks to the shore of the lake, letting her light play over the dark and still water. Scanning up and down the shoreline, nothing seems out of place. The gentle lapping of water against the rocky shoreline is the only sound interrupting the silence.

Chewing her lip, Kalisa glances over to the culvert. It's a large one, built to control floods and facilitate drainage for the entire area. Located at the end of a series of concrete channels, it's a foreboding sight—and the only place to hide in the extended flat ground around her. Tilting her head anxiously, she moves quietly toward it.

As Kalisa approaches, she stares into the darkness of its forbidding entrance. A large grate of metal bars covers the front of the hole, and a whisper of air whistles from its depths. As she gets close, she focuses down on an object in front of the metal barrier.

It's a golf shoe, and there's blood on its heel—smeared across the expensive white leather.

Trying to calm herself, Kalisa shines the light into the blackness beyond the bars. It's a big opening that descends into a dank area—behind bars a person couldn't possibly fit through. With her paltry light, she can't see into the recesses of the tunnel.

Standing still, Kalisa focuses for several long and silent moments. Far into the darkness, yellow eyes

CHAPTER FIVE

abruptly catch in the beam of her flashlight, then disappear just as fast.

"Oh, fuck this," says Kalisa, and she's had enough. Spinning around, she hurries back to the golf cart, her shoes squeaking as she trudges up the sloping embankment. Glancing warily back to the eerie culvert, she hopes reinforcements will soon arrive.

#

Several police lights twirl in the darkness, and a handful of patrol vehicles are parked around the culvert and driving range. Police tape has already been stretched around the stall where the golfer was playing, and a technician lowers his golf driver into a long clear bag.

At this remote part of the casino property, security guards keep curious onlookers from roaming too close to the area. Even at this time of day, a crowd is forming.

Near the lake, an odd-looking van is parked with "Search and Rescue" in bold lettering. Men in SCUBA gear carry equipment and bags to the shallows of the lake, and lights from searchers already underwater crisscross under the surface of the chilly water.

Kalisa stands back from the surge of police and technicians processing the crime scene, if it can be called that. She has her arms crossed in an annoyed gesture, looking ahead with an irritated scowl.

DESPICABLE

In front of her stands a police officer from the Reno Police Department. He has enormous bodybuilder muscles, and his custom-tailored shirt is made to show each crease of his pumped musculature. His lip is shrouded in an enormous mustache, as if he gets extra pay for growing the furry appendage. He's a guy who looks to have gotten into the law enforcement professional to stoke his ego—and for little else.

Kalisa leans forward to the man, not really trying to hide her contempt for his arrogant demeanor. She has a slight height advantage over the officer; for all his muscles, he doesn't seem to have inherited height from the genetic fairy. "I'm guessing you didn't graduate at the top of your academy class?"

The pompous cop regards her with a grin, ignoring her insult. He smacks a chaw of gum as he peers down at his notepad. "You say you saw eyes, like an animal, in that drainage area?"

Exasperated, Kalisa shakes her head and glances over to the culvert. Several cops are straining at the bars, trying to move the whole grate under the illumination of several cruiser headlights. With a joint grunt of victory, they manage to move the grate a few inches from its frame. Breathing deep, they let go of it and stand back with celebratory smiles.

Kalisa isn't impressed but manages to avoid saying anything. She rolls her eyes as she looks back to her interviewer.

CHAPTER FIVE

Muscle cop takes no notice of the other officers. He continues to smack his gum and adopts an intrigued tone as he continues writing. "So, I'm under the working theory that he went for a swim or decided to climb down into the sewers...or wherever that goes. Maybe he was drunk or under emotional stress?"

Kalisa shakes her head and scoffs. *What is it about bodybuilding that forces an IQ to drop?*

"So, this golfer dude, who was about a hundred pounds overweight, goes for a swim in the lake, after screaming and throwing his shoe over there," says Kalisa, and she becomes even more incredulous, letting her words drip with intentional sarcasm. "Or, he moves a gate aside that takes five of Reno's finest to barely budge...because he wants to drown himself in the sewers?"

Officer Flex frowns and snaps his notebook shut, looking up at Kalisa with a shit-eating grin. For the first time in her life, Kalisa wishes she had a machete to wipe that smile off someone else's face.

"Well, you're dismissed. Do let us know when you've solved this...missing person's case," he says, and he motions to several of Kalisa's coworkers, including Ben, who are pulling crowd control duties in back of her. "I'm sure you'll manage to pull it off with your elite jump team of investigators."

For a long moment, Kalisa and the officer meet eyes, and she fights the urge to move to open insults.

Turning away, Kalisa moves toward her colleagues, glad to join her friends—and normal people. As she paces their way, she lets slip a word, plenty loud for the cop to hear. "Prick."

#

Kalisa stands outside her door in the late afternoon light. She balances a load of late bills and requests for payment in one hand, while fiddling with an enormous set of keys in the other. Never one to throw away keys that might be of use one day, she frowns at the gaggle of clinking metal, wondering what the hell they'll actually open now.

Turning the lock, Kalisa enters the quiet apartment and throws the jumbled mail on the counter. Moving to the refrigerator, she stops briefly to gaze in pride at an award certificate for Seth, one that gave the boy first place in the *Nevada Chemistry Olympiad*. He stuck the award on the fridge months ago, and he still manages to derive happiness from his accomplishment every time he gets his milk or a snack.

Smiling, Kalisa pops the door open to gaze inside. Her eyes quickly come to rest on the eight-pack of beer on the top shelf, but she overcomes the urge to partake, looking away from the frosty brew with a frown. Opting instead for a carton of orange juice, she lets the door shut, still thinking about the beer as she fetches a glass from the cabinet.

CHAPTER FIVE

As she pours a tall serving, her eye catches on one of the envelopes stacked in the mess of letters she brought from the mailbox. She sets her glass aside and retrieves the brown envelope, pursing her lips in confusion at the somehow-familiar scrawl of "Kalisa Kinigi" above her address.

Opening the old-looking envelope reveals a simple sheet of paper, which looks yellowed, like it comes from some dusty old footlocker. When Kalisa unfolds the sheet, a check drops to the counter. She doesn't focus on the check, instead staring at the precise writing on the old paper.

Kalisa, remember who you are, and always do the right thing, wherever you are in life. I'll be waiting for you in heaven with your mother and brother.

Love,
Grandfather

Kalisa's eyes tear up at the words, so short and to-the-point they are written. She holds the paper for a long time, considering the wisdom from a man that had seen so much in life. She lays it down as she controls her breathing, stifling the urge to bawl like a child.

After Kalisa overcomes her foray into raw emotions, she holds up the check that had fallen from the middle of the short note. It's made out to her in the amount of five thousand dollars, to be drawn on the local bank where her grandpa had lived a hermit life over the last decade.

Breathing deep, Kalisa inserts the check and note back into the envelope. Placing her hands on the countertop, she taps the corner of it against the aged laminate, wondering what she should do with the unexpected inheritance.

#

Looking perplexed, Dr. Bergstrom leans back in his leather chair. He clicks a pen several times in his hand, mulling over his thoughts with a pained expression. "Did they find the man?"

In front of him, Kalisa paces the floor, and her deer-in-the-headlight face frowns in the gently lit therapy room. Stopping, she shakes her head and replays the recent memories of the incident involving the chubby golfer.

"The guy just disappeared," Kalisa says, and she plops in the seat, trying to get comfortable on the padded couch.

Rubbing her knuckles nervously, Kalisa tilts her head in confusion. "And I saw on the news that he had three kids and was loaded, with a pretty wife and big house. Why would he go anywhere?"

As confused as Kalisa, Bergstrom takes a moment to answer. Keeping his voice calm, he tries steering the conversation in another direction. "This is all very unfortunate—and tragic, if there is an unhappy ending to

CHAPTER FIVE

this poor man. But whether he ran off or harmed himself doesn't really have anything to do with you."

Kalisa looks unconvinced. "Doc, I'm not sure about that. I'm getting the feeling that someone…is following me, and now I'm the last person to see someone who disappeared?"

"I understand your worry…really, I do," responds Bergstrom, though he also appears a bit worried himself. "But let's ask ourselves: Who would want to hurt you or some random man at your work? You live a normal life."

"What about those eyes I saw in the tunnel? I'm not seeing things…am I?"

Bergstrom leans forward, managing to meet Kalisa's gaze, even as she tries to avoid his. His reassuring features soften even more, making her feel accepted and worthy. The doctor is like a real-life Santa for adults, and if ever there was a man born for this line of work, it's him.

After a silent nod, Bergstrom stands and moves to an ice bucket sitting on an end table in the corner of the room. Pulling a bottle of water from it, he hands it to Kalisa.

"Every kind of small—and some not so small—animals live here, even within the city limits," Bergstrom says. "It's the nature of this high desert that Reno was founded in."

When Kalisa takes a swig of the water, its coldness chills her throat, and she manages to feel hydrated despite the dry air in the office building. She licks her dry lips as Bergstrom continues.

"Small events in your life, and this is really no small event, can trigger any number of PTSD symptoms—."

"Like paranoia?" Kalisa interrupts.

Bergstrom nods. "Yes, even that. But…I think we have something else at play here. You were simply in the wrong place at the wrong time, and you are understandably blaming yourself. So, I want you to take care of yourself. Keep your outlook going forward, and don't allow peripheral events in your life to sidetrack you. It's essential for your well-being, and you deserve to be happy, Kalisa."

Kalisa is unsure of his words, but she appreciates his speech and good intentions. Standing, she paces to the middle of the room, where she raises her tone as she stretches her arms. "I've never imagined anything in my life, Doc, and now is no different. Something's wrong here, and I'm gonna find out what's going on."

A smile crosses Bergstrom's features, and he looks affectionately to Kalisa as he continues clicking his pen. But there's something else under the surface of his professional bearing: worry.

Shaking away his doubts, Bergstrom grins at Kalisa and motions to the clock. "There's nothing wrong with being sure of yourself. We'll talk about it more next Friday."

Chapter Six

The reception area of Baudin Funeral Home has been arranged to accept a larger crowd. Most of the couches have been moved out of it, leaving more space for mourners to mill around in the large space. Two tables of simple finger food are laid out at the end of the room, with pitchers of cheap juice and cheap beer offering liquid refreshment for a gathering crowd.

 The collection of people attending the memorial to Kalisa's grandfather is extensive and diverse. Wealthy-looking black immigrants of his age group, undoubtedly long-time acquaintances from the old country, mix with a collection of locals and simpler folk. A homeless guy even roams through the bright room, and it doesn't appear like he came for only the food, but to actually say goodbye. It's the celebration of life most would want, with people of all walks of life coming to see you off.

 On the wall that faces the entrance to the business is a large bulletin board, filled with all manner of photos of the elder Kinigi. In a line of pictures that start with him

DESPICABLE

in faded black-and-whites and end with more recent photographic fare, his life and evolution as a man are well-represented. In some of them, the normally serious man even shows a broad smile, made more notable by his white, beaming teeth.

Standing with her fingers intertwined, Kalisa smiles worriedly. She makes friendly eye contact with people she never knew, trying to play the part of a distraught family member, while at the same time trying to hide her shame at not keeping in touch with him over the years.

Looking to the front door, Kalisa is surprised when Darryl and Ben from work poke their heads in. She offers an appreciative smile and wave as they enter the room. The greeting is returned by both, and in Ben's case, he almost embarrasses the room with his happy and boisterous demeanor. He stops his waves at Kalisa when he notices the table of food and wades toward it.

Martin approaches Kalisa from a chat with another crowd of nameless faces to the back of the room. His demeanor cools, and he keeps his tone low while he leans close to his daughter. "It was a beautiful service. But…I find it strange that people he helped so much in his life couldn't see fit to attend his funeral."

Kalisa tries to keep her face pleasant as she considers her father's words. "Yeah…but maybe that's offset by people who owe him nothing, but came anyway?"

CHAPTER SIX

This gets a rare smile from Martin. "Touché, daughter. Perhaps it is not the quantity of admirers that matters in the end."

Kalisa allows herself a real grin as she feels the atmosphere improving, not having seen her dad's smile for a long time.

That's quickly cut short when Seth enters from the front entrance. Behind him is his dad, Rick Price. Rick is in his mid-thirties, white, and of average build. He has a kind face that's meant to smile, but he's not smiling now as he trails behind Seth.

Visibly upset, Kalisa walks forward to hug her son. Ignoring her affection, Seth points to the wall and the extensive photographic portfolio of his great-grandfather.

"Mom, Pappo looks even younger than dad there…and he was a soldier," exclaims Seth, gesturing to some pictures of the deceased in a military uniform.

"Yes, he was, Seth. He was a great man throughout his life," replies Kalisa, and she studiously avoids meeting her husband's eyes. "There was never a greater guy in the whole world."

From behind, Martin moves in and ushers Seth away from his mom and dad. Kalisa offers Martin an appreciative nod as they move toward the bulletin board to discuss the various snapshots of James' life.

DESPICABLE

Pivoting toward Rick, Kalisa approaches her husband carefully, not sure how to proceed. He greets her with steely eyes and a deadpan expression.

"Rick, how are you? I'm surprised you came inside. You didn't have to."

Breathing deep, Rick motions to the wall-of-life photos. "I know that, Kalisa. It would be rude to disrespect his celebration, even if he never liked me."

Kalisa tries to sound happy, though happiness is the furthest thing from her mind. "You're always welcome, you know that. And he never disliked you, he was just old-fashioned. He thought very highly of you, actually—he just wanted me to keep the traditions of the family."

Rick frowns and looks away, and for just a second Kalisa can see his wounded heart and destroyed pride—two things a man can never truly hide. Her heart breaks at the sight of it, knowing she's entirely responsible.

Rick looks back to Kalisa, lowering his voice so only she can hear. His eyes flash in anger. "Is your boyfriend welcome here, too? Or do you make it a point for him to be gone when I'm around?"

Kalisa's expression melts to sadness and internal embarrassment, and she's at a loss for words. She takes on the appearance of a death-row inmate, waiting to take her last walk. "That…person, is not in my life, and never will be again. *Never.*"

Kalisa certainly means that, but there's not a lot of good it will do now. It's not really helpful making good

CHAPTER SIX

decisions after you've made the stupidest ones on earth; you can't clean up after a hurricane with only a dustpan and broom.

Kalisa and Rick stare at each other for some time. With only silence between them, Rick nods and turns back to the entrance. As he leaves, Kalisa's jaw trembles, and she re-plasters an artificial smile over her distressed face as she turns back to the milling crowd.

#

The lights of Kalisa's humble car push through the darkness. The rattle of the worn springs and whine of her timing belt give the vehicle a wounded feeling, like it's an injured animal returning home to heal up.

Inside, Kalisa stares ahead at the road and familiar surroundings, but her mind is far removed from the present, with different emotions warring for control of her concerned face. Frustrated from her recent interactions with her husband and father, she barely notices the gaggle of kids hanging out in front of the parking lot. They step out of the way as she eases into her parking space.

In the back seat, Seth is less conflicted, and he looks happy, particularly for a kid that just attended a family funeral. His smile is even visible in the patchy darkness as Kalisa looks at him in the rear-view mirror.

Cheerful, Seth leans to the front seat and raises his voice enthusiastically. "Mom, I never knew Pappo was a war hero. I want one of those uniforms. Nobody at school will believe something this cool."

Kalisa grins as she climbs out of the car, taking time to collect some bags from the front seat. "I'll check with grandpa to see if it's okay, but don't tell your father on me. He'll think I'm making you into a war monger."

Seth continues his good mood, spilling from the car and running toward their building. A crowd of teens, including the obnoxious Eddie, parts quickly to let him through. Kalisa follows behind, and the group of young men avoid her gaze, finding anything else to look at.

Kalisa stops in the middle of the impromptu gang to stare at Eddie, who keeps his eyes elsewhere. He seems to have lost his smart-ass inclination, at least for the moment, and he continues avoiding her glare.

"Eddie," shouts Kalisa, and she allows a friendly smile to cross her face as she snaps a finger in front of his startled face.

Surprised, Eddie chances a look her way. "Uhh…yes, Mrs. Kinigi?"

"How are you today, Eddie? Are you having a good day? Doing well? Keeping out of trouble?"

The flurry of questions throws Eddie off. Wondering if it's a trick, he grows confused. "I'm okay, doing alright. Th…thanks for asking."

CHAPTER SIX

Eddie's pals are all quiet, not knowing how to respond or what to say. When Kalisa also sweeps them with her kind gaze, each appears uncomfortable, like they'd rather be somewhere else.

Kalisa claps Eddie firmly on the shoulder, like they're old friends. The sudden movement makes the entire group flinch, and for a moment there's an expectant silence.

"Good," says Kalisa, and with a warm nod she paces off toward her apartment. Clambering up the stairs, she feels a bit better about the world, like she finally did something right. Stopping at the top, she glances back for a last measure of the teens.

But her gaze falters as she moves her eyes to the curb outside her complex, where an expensive Mercedes is parked. As she focuses on the out-of-place vehicle in the gritty neighborhood, its lights go out, but nobody exits.

Staring for several moments, she finally tears her eyes away from the silent car. Frowning, she enters her modest apartment.

Behind, the boys watch her enter with relieved expressions, unaware of the suspicious vehicle behind them. Some even smile, especially Eddie, as if they just made a new friend.

DESPICABLE

Kalisa sits propped in her bed in the dim light of her room. Several pillows are piled around her, and a fluffy comforter covers her legs on the king-size bed. With her small size and the array of blankets, she looks like she's swimming in a cozy cotton sea.

The walls of the room around her have several photo frames, and most of them show Seth in various poses, from soccer player to aspiring chemistry researcher. Two have her husband's photo, but one of those frames has a shattered glass cover, like it had been thrown against the wall at some point. Kalisa frowns as she looks at it, making a mental note get it replaced.

Looking down at her phone, Kalisa begins to tap on the bright screen.

THANKS FOR COMING TONIGHT. HOW ARE YOU DOING?

The app on her phone lists the recipient as "Rick." It shows a colored check mark to indicate he's received the text, and his status subsequently changes several times, revolving between "typing" and "online."

Kalisa waits for a response, praying that he will see fit to acknowledge her. *I can only make this right, Rick, if you let me make it up to you. Somehow.*

The text standoff continues for a while more, and Kalisa's hopes increase. *Just please answer me.*

But Rick doesn't answer, and his virtual indicator goes off without a response. Kalisa continues watching her screen, even though she knows he won't be coming back.

CHAPTER SIX

He may never come back, and if he's smart, he won't look back. God, I'm a dumbass.

Kalisa drops the phone on her covers and smacks herself on the forehead with her palm several times, mocking her own stupidity. She's never been in a situation where she had to try to win someone back, so it's unfamiliar territory, and the fact that she's mistreated the one man who did everything for her makes her more desperate. It's all on her, and if she fails, it's Seth that'll pay the price of her infidelity—a cost born by weekends with dad and a chaotic home life without stability.

Frustrated, Kalisa rolls over, mulling her past and focusing on her future as she stares at her chipped-paint bedroom wall. Pulling her covers tight, she tries to force the angst to leave her thoughts, bit by precious bit. Focusing inside, she pushes away her fears and shame, making her muscles relax against the constant noise of interior trauma that's made a home in her head. As her breaths deepen, sleep pulls her downward, and she shifts into her wretched dreams.

Young Kalisa peered from beneath the shadowy confines of her neighbor's porch. The home above her was simple and clean, and its recessed basement windows allowed an expansive view of the afternoon street outside. Her eyes were terrified, assuming the wide-eyed look of abject fear.

The day outside would have been nice, if not for the bodies, some bloated and others recently butchered, that sprawled on the dirt street

DESPICABLE

in front of the house. Pools of blood and unnamable gore leaked from the various neighbors she had known all her life.

Abruptly, a crowd of revelers came into view. Cheering at the heaps of corpses that litter the street, their joy at wanton murder was otherworldly and demonic. One-by-one the demented people collected the bodies, punctuating their wicked enjoyment of the moment with odd chants and exhortations.

Kalisa's eyes fell upon the ghastly scene, focusing on the gathering heaps of corpses. Her view fixated on one of the dead in particular, her grandmother. Her beautiful Nanna was oddly contorted at the bottom of the pile, and her open eyes stared at Kalisa, like she couldn't figure how to extricate herself from that odd, contorted position.

Several of the heinous celebrants brought forward cans of gasoline. They splashed the pungent fuel on the dead, drenching the mound of deceased with several gallons of the stuff. Kalisa was able to see the liquid pour over her grandmother's face, clearing away her blood-streaked death stare, if only for a moment.

The heap of humanity was lit, and the flames licked across the broken flesh of the dead. As the fire moved down to consume her Nanna, the horrid odor of the burning people leaked into Kalisa's hiding spot, along with some fetid smoke, forcing Kalisa to turn away from the scene.

Kalisa's youthful face and mind lost touch with reality, and she assumed the distant stare of a person who would never again process the world in the same way.

CHAPTER SIX

Coming awake, Kalisa takes a moment to focus, her eyes reassuming their grasp on the present. The room around her is still dimly lit, with nobody else to bear witness to her horrid dreams from so long ago.

Sitting up, Kalisa looks at her phone, noting it is 3:12 AM. Feeling overwhelmed, she puts her face in her hands. Trembling, she sobs in her lonely bedroom, dealing with her pain as she always has—by herself.

Chapter Seven

The gym's hardscrabble interior has two fighting rings, and spaced inside the rest of the business is a multitude of heavy and light punching bags, along with a large mat for wrestling. Thirty people exercise throughout the area, punching and kicking at one another as they practice varied martial arts.

Kalisa holds her gloved hands up, peering intently across the ring. She breaths in rasps, and a thick sheen of sweat covers her face, soaking her form-fitting tank-top. Across from her, Steven, a fit man in his thirties, holds up two separate black leather pads, waiting for her to move in.

With a shout Kalisa rushes forward, kicking with several THWACKS in quick succession. She grunts from the considerable effort, turning her hips to get more leverage in each blow. Across from her, Steven moves fast, adjusting the arc and timing with his hands, allowing her to practice her accuracy to full effect.

Switching to punches, Kalisa launches a series of hard strikes into the rapidly moving pads. For twenty blows she continues, using all her strength to land each jarring impact into the hard leather. As she slams each punch into her imagined opponent, she works into a heightened frenzy, like she's clobbering the devil himself.

Stopping, Kalisa finds herself heaving for air, and she leans against the ropes to catch her breath. Glancing over to her training partner, she continues gasping as she meets Steven's smiling face.

"Good workout," Steven says, and he removes his padded gloves with a smirk. "You seem wound up today."

Kalisa smiles, still trying to get breath into her lungs. As her heart slows to a more normal pace, she nods in appreciation to Steven, who chuckles and exits the ring.

Staring down at her boxing gloves, Kalisa removes them by prying off their velcro straps. Setting them aside, she stretches as she cools down from her training, rotating her shoulders and arms in a windmill fashion to loosen up from the flurry of aggressive movements.

Just then, a man entering the front of the gym catches her eye. Detective Wiggins lets the door close with a methodical click as he stands there, like being quiet has some benefit in the noisy gym.

In his forties, Wiggins has an affable smile and a stocky stature. He wears an ancient sport coat, one with patches that cover his elbows, and he exudes a clinical

CHAPTER SEVEN

and focused temperament as he scans the gym, looking for someone.

Walking close to the ring, Wiggins' eyes and face light up as he recognizes Kalisa. He greets her with a slight bow. "Looks like we have the next Joe Louis in the house."

Kalisa cocks her head as she recalls the man's face. With a half-smile, she speaks in a guarded voice, spacing her words out cautiously. "That's…boxing. This is Muay Thai."

"Well then, I shouldn't comment on things I know nothing about," replies Wiggins, and he switches to a friendly manner, trying to be polite. "How are you, Kalisa?"

Not answering, Kalisa climbs between the ropes and exits the boxing ring. Stepping close to Wiggins, she looks down at her hand wraps, unsure if she should shake with the sweaty strips of cloth.

Wiggins grins and shows he doesn't care by jutting out his hand in greeting. They clasp in a strong shake, measuring each other up with pleasant expressions.

Kalisa remembers the man but takes a while to consider what he would be doing here. "I've been better. How about you, detective?"

Wiggins smiles knowingly, nodding in understanding. "OK, I guess, but I get this missing person's case crossing my desk, and it's got me flustered. Takes me a while to make any sense out of it. Then, lo and behold, whose name do I see as the witness—the last person to see the guy before he disappears?"

Kalisa ignores the question. "You're working missing persons now? I thought you did background investigations?"

Wiggins shakes his head, opening his arms to indicate the wide area of the city. "This is Reno. It isn't like we got the numbers for specialized departments. My boss must have thought I could find the dude. Hope he's not wrong."

Kalisa lowers her eyes at the mention of the department and her unique position as a last witness. She's well aware that "last witness", usually means "prime suspect." Becoming a suspect is neither fair nor logical, but it is what it is.

Wiggins' smile becomes strained. He adopts an apologetic tone and lowers his voice. "I'm sorry we didn't take you on at the department. Your scores and fitness level were great, but—."

"My gambling and drinking scared you off," says Kalisa, finishing his words. "I read the background report. Several times, in fact."

Wiggins scowls a bit, perhaps not liking having words put in his mouth, even if they're true. "Well, those things aren't permanently disqualifying, Kalisa. You can reapply when they are…less recent."

"I'll do that someday, detective, but I'll be drawing social security by the time the department takes that risk.

CHAPTER SEVEN

Apparently, the force only wants people that have no life and zero experience facing real-world problems."

That came out harsher than Kalisa intended, and she takes a deep breath to control her emotions. Still, it's how she feels, so...*fuck 'em if they don't like the truth.*

There's an awkward moment of silence, interrupted by grunts from two men grappling on a mat a few yards away.

"What brings you here?" asks Kalisa, looking back to Wiggins.

"Well, we're looking for the missing golfer and don't have a clue about his whereabouts. Except for a bloody shoe, he's disappeared. Thought I would check in with you and get your thoughts."

Kalisa shakes her head, equally unsure of what happened. "The whole thing is crazy. As I told that dipshit Jackson—."

"Johnson," interrupts Wiggins.

"Johnson," says Kalisa, clearly uninterested in getting the name of the pompous cop right. "It doesn't make any sense. What happy, rich guy kills himself by jumping into a golf lake?"

Wiggins agrees with a nod. "We had divers check out the whole lake. Nothing there except beer bottles and carp."

Pursing her lips, Kalisa begins unwrapping her hands. Her eyes lock with Wiggins as she makes her next words clear and deliberative. "I definitely saw a set of eyes—there must have been an animal in that culvert tunnel."

"I've toyed with the theory that it might be an animal attack. But in the middle of the city, with no remains after searching with dogs, it just doesn't feel right. I'm getting the feeling there's something we missed."

Kalisa takes a deep breath and shakes her head. Reaching down, she begins packing a workout bag with her various equipment. "I guarantee you you're missing something...but there isn't much I can do to help. I guess that's why you get the big bucks."

Hefting her bag, Kalisa motions towards the women's locker room, indicating their conversation has run its course. Wiggins tags along as she strides towards the door.

Turning back, Kalisa offers her hand in another shake, and they clasp in an awkward goodbye. She holds his hand a bit longer than before—noticeably longer than he wants.

"Before you go," says Kalisa, and she cocks her head while keeping her firm handshake. "Are you having me followed? I've noticed several cars tailing me lately."

Wiggins furrows his brow, considering the question. Kalisa notes his skeptical look and is somewhat relieved.

"You know if I did, I couldn't tell you," answers Wiggins. "But there's no way we can afford to tail...innocent witnesses."

CHAPTER SEVEN

Kalisa releases his hand, nodding as she thinks over his answer. She doesn't much like the way he said the word "innocent," like it was an open question. But still, he appears honest and sincere. She's spent a lifetime smelling bullshit, and she's not getting that same vibe from Wiggins now.

Flashing Wiggins a faint smile, Kalisa turns and walks through the locker-room door.

#

The flamboyant apartment is lit by neon bulbs running the length of its ceiling, throwing a different hue of colored light every few feet. Above a timeworn leather couch in the living room is a garish print of Jimi Hendrix, who jams at a crowd of partying hippies in front of several old-fashioned peace signs. The other walls are empty of decorations, except for smudges of grease and long-unwashed grime on their old paint.

The rest of the place could also use a sprucing up, as a veneer of dust seems to have overtaken the once-present shine on various wooden furniture. Light leaks through some wrinkled curtains on the front of the apartment, while the beat of music from Morrissey drifts from a hallway at the back of the apartment. The incessant whining of the aged singer seems appropriate for the depressing mood of the living area.

Walking from the dark hallway, Eddie stops and frowns as he considers something. Rubbing his stomach, he focuses on the kitchen and moves to an old refrigerator humming in the corner.

When Eddie eases the fridge open, he's greeted by several boxes of takeout Chinese, surrounded by a gallon of milk and a hodgepodge of cheap condiments. Some dried and not very appetizing-looking fruits sit on the bottom shelf, waiting to be thrown out. The rest of the cold storage is bereft of edible fare, so Eddie grabs a carton of the Asian food and moves to the counter.

Cracking open the container, Eddie moves to smell the delectable meal, but his quest for culinary enjoyment is answered by a foul odor, and he drops the box with a sour look. Sighing, Eddie peers expectantly around the dim apartment, as if a pizza might fall from the sky to address his hunger issues.

A knock on the front door answers his hopeful gaze, and Eddie becomes confused as he considers who it could be. Hesitantly, he walks to the door and cracks it open.

Outside, Kalisa looks at him through the opening. She is smiling, almost carefree in her appearance, as she peers at him through the crack. Eddie drops his gaze, instantly worried. *What did I do now?*

"My mom isn't here right now," says Eddie, and his voice takes on a whiny tone. "She won't be home for a while. Please don't tell her about the other night."

CHAPTER SEVEN

Kalisa clucks her tongue and shakes her head, trying her best *I'm your best friend* imitation. "Eddie, that's ancient history. We all make mistakes; the important thing is that we LEARN from them. Can I come in?"

Eddie nods and steps out of the way as he swings the door in. He isn't exactly enthusiastic, but his former scowl drops off. "So, what do you want, then?"

Kalisa scoots past him in the doorway, taking her time to appraise the unkempt apartment before returning her gaze to Eddie. She offers him a sympathetic nod before continuing. "I need you to do me a favor."

Eddie's face returns to his worried state, mixed with apprehension. He stays quiet.

"On the street in front of the complex are two cars—an Audi and a Mercedes," says Kalisa, and she motions out the still-open door. "In about an hour, can you go for a walk down the street and take a photo of their license plates for me? Don't be obvious about it; I need you to act like a secret agent with this."

Kalisa holds out her phone, an expensive one. "You can use my phone."

Eddie looks doubtful, and his confusion only grows as he chews on his lip.

Kalisa recognizes his hesitancy, and she moves in to seal the deal. "And, I'll give you twenty bucks."

The mention of money lights a fire in the eyes of the otherwise substance-affected teen. He leans in a bit, for the first time seeming interested. "What about fifty?"

DESPICABLE

Kalisa smiles broadly. "Forty, and the next time you and your friends need to go somewhere, I'll take you—no matter where or when. But you have to wait until payday for the cash."

Eddie smiles, eyes wide and happy. For once, Kalisa can see the shy and hopeful boy underneath the punk exterior—exactly the guy she knew was hiding.

#

The back of the funeral home is surprisingly large, like it could be a loading dock for some sprawling big-box store. Four channeled concrete lanes move from the road that circles the business toward large roll-up doors along the back wall, all of which are closed in the dim twilight cast down from the starry night. It's an industrial-sized operation for whatever delivery needs the funeral business requires.

In the confines of the back dock, along an interior area shielded from outside, stands Mathias Baudin. His face is serious in the scant light, and he stares into the darkness, waiting for something.

A semi with tractor-trailer abruptly pulls into view, working its gears and banking away from the lane leading to Mathias' loading area. Strangely, the large vehicle is without lights or means for seeing in the dark. Even more odd, it moves with reckless speed, and it barrels in reverse toward Mathias with a masterful show of driving skill. No

CHAPTER SEVEN

sounds of beeping or warning lights accompany the maneuver, and with little room to spare on either side, it squeaks to a halt within inches of the lip of the dock.

Mathias reaches back and gently taps the metal doors. He is quickly rewarded with the barrier being raised, but unlike typical doors, there's little sound from the movement, as if its tracks are greased to silent perfection.

Two men emerge from the murk of the interior, quickly opening the truck's rear door and moving inside. Over the next several minutes, the men ferry dark boxes from the cargo space into the building. They use no flashlights, yet they have no trouble negotiating the confines of the trailer or the inside of the facility as they stack their delivery.

At peace with the unloading operation, Mathias steps from the shadows, moving into the night's vague light. A barely visible smile crosses his contented lips, and he looks into the night sky, breathing in the refreshing air as he ponders the surroundings of his business.

When the workers have completed the offload of goods, they disappear inside the building itself. After a while, they return dragging separate handcarts with scores of boxed caskets stacked on them. On each of the crated boxes is stenciled "FRAGILE." Efficiently, they load them onto the truck, ensuring they are properly packed for transportation and never missing a beat in their cadenced and calm movements.

DESPICABLE

When everything is loaded and cinched inside, the men drop the vehicle's door with only the slightest of clanks. Mathias stares disapprovingly at the noise, and the workers nod sheepishly before returning to their former perch inside the building. The loading-dock door is lowered without further audible intrusion into the peaceful night.

Mathias sighs as he considers the night around him, sweeping his eyes over the building and property with focused precision. Looking ahead, he moves toward the cab of the truck.

Standing below the enormous cab, his bearing is confident as he stares up into the dark interior, where the shadowy silhouette of the driver gazes back at him. Mathias pulls out an envelope from his heavy coat and hands it to the driver, who accepts it with only the mildest of nods.

Pivoting, Mathias strides back to his building, a place that remains lightless in the dark. He enters through a regular door into the dock area, clicking it shut as he disappears inside.

Outside, the gently idling semi lurches into gear and accelerates into the darkness, gathering speed as it moves past the corner of the private driveway towards the main road. When it reaches the threshold of public streetlights there, lights on its cab and trailer turn on, and it's soon lost down the thoroughfare of the industrial area as it merges with other traffic.

CHAPTER SEVEN

#

The gun range is well lit, with several bright lights running the length of the indoor facility. A series of ten separate lanes occupy the interior, with dividers keeping each of the firing positions somewhat private from each other. Cables run down the ceiling of each of the lanes, allowing for targets to be run back and forth from the firing positions to different distances with an electronic switch.

Lance Ericsson stands at lane *1*, peering down at his target with a grimace. In his thirties, cocky, and good-looking, he shakes his head at the results on his man-silhouette target fifteen yards down the range. Dressed in a police uniform, he has the presence of someone who gets what he wants, when he wants.

Holding up a semi-automatic pistol, "Made in Croatia" is visible on the side of the impressive-looking black weapon. Lance inserts a magazine into it and racks the weapon's slide forward. Setting it aside for a moment, he moves smoothly and begins loading .40 caliber ammunition into other magazines from a box of bullets on the lane's tray table. As he tops up each of the spare clips, he smiles and places them in a methodical order, getting ready for his next round of shooting.

Pulling his ear protection down and focusing through his off-colored goggles, Lance assumes a firing stance as he aims his pistol, looking a bit like an alien stormtrooper. When he begins blasting away, each of the shots punches a hole in his target, with the head and torso of his paper victim quickly filling with the marks of his shots.

His weapon empty, Lance presses the switch that returns the target with a whir of the pulleys it's attached to. Examining the placement of his rounds, he takes a second to enjoy the superiority of his marksmanship, and a *Good God, I am good* smile crosses his handsome features. The acrid smell of discharged ammunition doesn't lessen his self-important moment of personal glory.

A few lanes down from him, another shooter begins blasting away. The caliber of the unseen weapon provides less of a pop when firing, but the results are the same on the shooter's target: the paper is perforated with holes in all the important areas.

After the other shooter stops, Lance nods, thoroughly impressed. He raises his voice, speaking unintentionally loudly, as he still wears his hearing protection. "Good shooting. I don't see that kind of skill very often."

From behind the dividers between them, Kalisa's raised voice answers the compliment. "Thanks, I've had lots of practice."

Surprised, Lance sets down his pistol and steps back to get a view of this new firing-line participant to the side. His astonished eyes go wide.

Laying down her 9 MM Ruger pistol and safety headset, Kalisa faces him and stares back. She crosses her arms and raises an eyebrow as she meets his gaze. "Hello, Lance."

CHAPTER SEVEN

At first, Lance is ecstatic to see Kalisa. Then, some worry fills his face as he considers what her presence here could mean. "Hi Kalisa, it's been a while. I…wasn't expecting to see you here."

"Nice to see you, too," Kalisa responds, and she takes a step forward, lowering her tone as she keeps his gaze. "I called the precinct to find you, and they said you were here. So, here I am."

There's a moment of silence, and it's obvious from his scowl Lance doesn't like her calling his workplace. From Kalisa's own playful stare, she clearly could care less what he likes.

Puzzling over the direction of this encounter, Lance takes a deep breath, trying to look hopeful. "Are you here to reconsider my…um offer?"

Kalisa shakes her head curtly, taking another step toward the suddenly unsure cop. "No, not interested in being your girlfriend, Lance. I'm here for something else."

Lance finally takes off his goggles and ear protection, setting them aside and sighing as he readjusts to the developing conversation. He's disappointed at having his relationship offer spurned, but he wears a face that's accustomed to finding new girlfriends…with little trouble. They both know it.

Kalisa gets to the point of her visit. "I need you to do me a favor. I have two license plate numbers," she says, and she pulls out her phone, scrolling through some

DESPICABLE

photos on her screen, "And I need you to look them up. Get me the names and addresses of the owners."

It's Lance's turn to cross his arms, and hope and kindness have left his demeanor. "Well, this is interesting. You cut off our relationship with no warning, and now you want me to maybe get in trouble?"

"Our 'relationship' involved empty sex at your discretion—hardly the stuff of romance novels."

Lance frowns, not liking her accurate appraisal of their prior escapades. "OK, but it meant something to me—,"

"Cut the bullshit," says Kalisa, and her features grow sad for a moment. "I threw away my marriage for those ridiculous nights...together. And that's on me, all my fault. But now, I need this information; it's very important."

Lance shakes his head, adopting a virtuous whine. "What you want me to do is called browsing, and it could get me fired. I can't...won't...do that."

Kalisa grins up at him, but there's no mirth in her face. "We met when you pulled me over, and you offered me a date to get out of the ticket. I'm pretty sure I'm not the only woman to be rewarded with your generosity, and I'm also certain that could get you fired."

Lance takes a step back, looking surprised, like a boy caught doing something wrong—but not understanding why he's being punished for it. No response as the gears turn in his mind, trying to find a way out of this shakedown.

CHAPTER SEVEN

Kalisa moves in for the kill. "So, unless you want your bosses or the news to know about it, get your phone out and find me the information I need. Time is a-wastin'."

Lance's expression melts into terrified worry. After an extended stare down, he nods reluctantly.

Showing him a conciliatory grin, Kalisa pats him gently on the chest, picking at his name tag with false affection. "And I promise…I'll never bother you again."

Chapter Eight

The living room is filled with marijuana smoke, enough to make seeing fully across it a chore. Scattered through the space are soda bottles and cartons of half-eaten pizza, showing something like heaven for slacking teens and unambitious louts.

On the wall is a large 75-inch television, placed perfectly to allow a wide-angle view from the whole of the room. An assemblage of teens lay sprawled on a ratty couch and chairs around it, staring up at the enormous screen.

On the TV, a computer-graphic soldier creeps to the edge of a building. As he peers over the lip, he sees several armed men with AK-47's lounging on a patio across the street. Staying low, the sniper focuses on the group, getting into a precise location and getting ready for the shot.

As the reticule of the sniper's bolt-action rifle focuses on one of the creepy-looking Middle Eastern guy, the sniper zooms further on his head. With a crack, the man's head explodes, and the terrorist crumples out of view.

The sniper ducks down on the roof, just as a fusillade of return fire peppers the wall and roof around him.

An overweight stoner friend jumps from the couch, celebrating with a "Yessss" and pumping his arm in what's probably his only exercise for the day. A filthy and loose shirt printed with the images of "Beavis and Butthead" matches his ungroomed and slouched stature. "Dude, you got 'em. Good shot."

Extricating himself from a large beanbag in the middle of the room, Eddie stands and drops a game controller. A hodgepodge of youthful friends around him stare up like he's the gaming messiah.

"You just gotta move into position slowly," says Eddie, playing the role of reluctant genius. "If they hear ya comin', they always waste you before you can take the shot. It's all about patience…and perseverance."

Stoner reaches down and grabs a joint perched on a well-used ashtray. He takes a hit, his eyes lulling further into subdued contentment. Smoke rolls from his unhygienic mouth as he processes the effects on his foggy brain. Holding it out, he bids Eddie to join him in baked bliss. "Dude, your turn. My brother scored the good stuff…just like always."

Eddie peers down at the spliff, thinking over its benefits as he focuses on the spit-drenched end of the poorly rolled blunt. Suddenly, Stoner's familial pride at

CHAPTER EIGHT

procuring dope doesn't strike him as a particularly worthy achievement. In fact, even the constant video games are starting to lose their attraction, along with the smelly clothes he finds himself playing in every day.

Eddie shakes his head slowly, coming to a surprising conclusion. "Nah, thanks, man. I gotta get home. Tomorrow I'm gonna have a job interview. That donut place really wants to hire me."

The room around Eddie goes silent. The mouths of his friends are open, their eyes staring in rapt shock, like the Beelzebub himself just proclaimed himself a Baptist.

Stoner is only able to utter a simple syllable, his hand still extending the marijuana offering. "Huh?"

Eddie glances around the room, feeling embarrassed—but somehow empowered. "Guys, this is fun, but I gotta make some money—get a life. We can't just play games and smoke weed the rest of our lives."

The continuing silence and exasperated expressions of his buddies offer an unspoken question: *why not?*

Shaking his head, Eddie shirks into his coat while the room remains quiet. Reaching down, he grabs his backpack and slings it onto his shoulders as the stares around him continue.

Smiling and nodding, Eddie saunters out the front door. As it clicks shut behind him, the group stares at each other, trying to process their good friend's shocking heresy.

Eddie walks with purpose down a leafy city street. Streetlights illuminate the darkness around him every few yards, and the night sky casts hazy moonlight through a collection of scattered clouds above.

There's a bounce in Eddie's step, and a strange sense of pride pulses through his body, like he's suddenly a superhero, doing what he always should have done. A beaming smile fills his face as he jaunts his way past collections of family homes and finely trimmed lawns.

Ahead, the vague street outline continues on, stabbing into the heart of a pleasant suburban landscape, with the silhouettes of SUVs and trucks parked along the curb providing sporadic reminders of a sedate and safe environment.

Further on, there's a break in the road, and a small lane detaches to the right. Here, the road is gravelly, and it twists back into the darkness with only the murky glow of starry night to probe its depths. To the side of this backwoods pathway, there are a plethora of trees that hug the track, leaning at odd angles to create a dense thicket on each side of the pathway.

Eddie knows this way well; it's a path he's taken often in his young life, cutting back and forth and saving time over the regular route to visit friends. He changes direction into the darkness without hesitation and strides

CHAPTER EIGHT

ahead, still feeling a buoyant mood over the possibilities in his near future. *Life is good.*

As Eddie moves along, he thinks about his mom, a woman that for all her strange ways has really given him everything. His dad was a dirtbag, leaving them to fend for themselves all his life, and even a couple trips to the county jail over unpaid child support wasn't enough to get money from that loser's meth-addled fingertips.

All the while his mom labored away in the casinos, working multiple shifts cleaning shitters, while at the same time avoiding the vices surrounding her. It was all for his sake, to keep him well fed and with a roof over his head. Eddie never thought too deeply about the role of parental responsibility in the world, particularly as it pertains to him, but now he kinda understands just what she does for him.

Maybe that's why his recent foray into sobriety matters, Eddie realizes. If he continues down the road of drugs, even the mild stuff, maybe life won't ever get better for him and his mom. Maybe he could even take a few classes at the college after high school and get a real job. Maybe, just maybe, he could help her a bit then. She must get tired of cleaning crap and breathing casino smoke. God knows he could never do that work.

Eddie stops for a second, thinking some more. What do people really have to look forward to if they can't take care of their family, especially when it's really needed?

DESPICABLE

All of this altruism running through his veins is something new for Eddie, and his grin grows to gargantuan proportions. He scours the woods around him, as if someone might be there to witness the first time in his life he thought about someone other than himself.

Unfortunately, nobody's there to notice his good intentions or to praise his conscience.

Farther on, the silent woods to his right sway mildly with a breeze, bringing a chill to Eddie. Pulling his coat tighter, he refocuses and walks on, concentrating on a break in the trees where the road moves through it. *For my first paycheck, I'm gonna get mom a big set of roses; she always liked those.*

Farther to the right, there's a rustling in the bushes, just enough to get his attention. Eddie stops, suddenly unsure of himself. He can't see anything, but the hairs on his neck wake up in a tingling moment of trepidation. *What…?*

Not liking the feeling, Eddie moves his gaze to the road in front of him. He quickens his pace as he tries to recapture the feeling of optimism that so recently made a home in his mind. Instead, a percolating sense of dread washes through his guts, and now he really just wants to get home.

From the darkness up ahead, the creature watches Eddie, taking in his youthful glow in the shadowy night. As Eddie moves toward it, its stare falls on his neck, where the increase in blood flow caused by his fear rushes just under the skin. The THUMP of his

CHAPTER EIGHT

heart grows faster, and as Eddie gets closer to the woods, the creature steps near the edge of the road. Getting closer.

Eddie stops in the dirt street, again focusing on the forested area. Staring into the gaps of the trees, his growing sense of terror surges, forcing him into an apoplectic stupor. He's just able to make out the outlines of the creature, with its silhouette made more clear with each passing moment. Its yellow eyes grow more pronounced as they focus on him.

Eddie concentrates into the confines of the brush and trees. It looks almost like a man, but its elongated arms seem oddly out of sync in the darkness. *What the fuck?*

Eddie raises his hand to point at the creature, as if noticing the creature in the thickets will be less menacing by his sudden attention. For a moment, there's an imagined standoff as neither he nor the creature move.

The silence is broken when a black-clawed hand grabs Eddie's neck from behind, and he's pulled from his feet with a "Yelp."

The creature in the woods watches Eddie struggle on the ground, and its yellow eyes appear indifferent to the sound of the unseen fight between Eddie and its animalistic companion. The rest of the creature's face isn't visible, but those large yellow eyes focus from the shadows, unblinking and cat-like.

"Ahhhh...help...urgh" screams Eddie, and claws from the dark humanoid form tear into him. The shadowed beast above him rips out his throat, and gore

DESPICABLE

sprays in spurts across the dusty rocks and matted earth of the untraveled road. Panting for air, Eddie gurgles and spits up gouts of blood, unable to understand what's happening. A choking gasp is the only thing that escapes his torn mouth and ravaged throat.

In a moment, it's over, and Eddie's limp arms, held up in a vain attempt at defense, flop to the ground. His eyes adjust their stare into the night sky, becoming vacant as his heaving chest stops moving. Thoughts of his mother and a hopeful future leave his mind, along with all other worldly considerations. Everything that Eddie ever was or could be is now gone.

Moving quietly, his attacker grabs Eddie by his matted hair and yanks him to the side. Lurching toward the trees, it drags him into the dry brush and thorns of thick bushes. When it moves across a beam of moonlight, the man-sized frame of the dark figure with long arms is revealed.

As it strides into the depths of the woods, it is joined by the other creature, and for a moment something else is visible from the duo: Each creature is wearing tattered overalls, with dark short-sleeve shirts, and dark leather boots on their strange frames.

Not looking back, both creatures pad into the constricted shrubs and trees, pulling their young victim behind them.

#

CHAPTER EIGHT

Travis Sproles stands at the window of the quiet office, deeply enmeshed in his personal thoughts. With a cheap suit covering his athletic frame, the thirty-something frowns as he sips from an enormous mug, rolling the lukewarm liquid under his pursed lips. The mug's lettering approaches profound philosophy with "She's Even Uglier" scrawled in faded lettering on its worn and coffee-stained exterior.

Peering from one of the upper floors of a high-rise building, he looks over meandering traffic below in the Washington, DC sprawl. The view is expansive and pleasant, with the scattered and beeping vehicles looking like marching bugs under the afternoon's wilting light.

Dropping his scowl, Travis turns and walks to the door that leads into his small office. There doesn't appear to be anyone to witness his work, but he still peeks his head out to ensure no nosy interlopers can bother him at the end of his workday.

In the collection of desks outside, there's nobody else evident, and only the distant buzz of someone's too-loud television provides evidence that the office is even occupied.

Moving to his desk and plopping in his seat, Travis puts on some glasses and squints at this computer monitor. The room is scantly lit, and as the monitor buzzes to life, the reflection on his lenses shows a colorful screen with columns of numbers and highlighted words. Travis grimaces at the unseen screen, pulling a notepad close and writing extensively. From his serious demeanor, the subject of his attention should be important and mind-engrossing—truly important stuff.

Sighing, Travis circles something on the pad paper and drops the pen, his face growing flushed in frustration. He drums his fingers on the desk, pondering intensely as he wrinkles his face. Finally, he comes to a decision.

Glancing again at the monitor, he removes his glasses and focuses on the wording there, trying to decide how he can see better with or without reading enhancement. On the computer are several betting lines from various contests, with spreads for an array of games across several different sports in bolded fonts.

On his notepad is written, "Los Angeles +11". Nodding to himself, Travis runs his index finger over his circled prognostication. Clicking on a spot to make a bet on the screen, he begins to fill out personal information to make his bet go live. When he gets to a field that demands his credit card number, he stands to pull out his wallet from a front pocket.

Just then, his phone rings, with AC/DC providing an attractive ringtone from his mobile lying on his desk. Travis glances at his cheap phone with an irritated huff. He sighs as he grabs it, taking a deep breath before speaking.

"Yeah? Agent Sproles here."

Lance's voice greets him from the other side of the country. "Dude, it's me. What's going on?"

CHAPTER EIGHT

"Lance," says Travis, and his face fills with a smile, one reserved for old friends. "Haven't heard from you since that conference...last November, right?"

"Yeah, that was a crazy trip. You and Dawkins were so fucking drunk I thought we'd have to bail you out the next morning. Good thing the security guards didn't get us all in trouble. I think you guys caught the plane with more booze in your bodies than blood."

Nodding, Travis' smile grows even more pronounced. "Yeah, if only we had more times like that to liven up our lives...shit gets boring in an office all day."

The connection grows silent, and Travis wonders what's coming next. He lowers his voice, sounding intrigued. "This doesn't sound like a call to reminisce about drinking or high school. What's up?"

"Yeah, well...I got something I hope you can help me with. I'm trying to run plates on some cars I came across."

"You run NCIC more than I do, bro," Travis replies. "Why call me?"

"It's weird, the plates come back as 'restricted,' which makes no sense. Not even Fed vehicles do that. If I text 'em to you, can you check it out and get back to me?"

Interested, Travis tilts his head as he considers the problem. "Yeah, sure, send them over. I'll look into it."

"Thanks, dude. And...can you do one other thing for me?" asks Lance.

"Yeah?"

DESPICABLE

"Quit betting those shitty Parlays. Just Paypal me your money when you're feeling too rich. At least that way, one of us can enjoy your wasted cash."

"Fuuuuuccck you, bro."

Hanging up, Travis chuckles and sits down again. As he opens some programs on his screen, he reaches into his desk and takes out a scrap of paper. While he's entering passwords from the paper, his phone lights up with several text messages from Lance.

Fully logged in, Travis enters the data from the phone into his systems. After several taps on his keyboard, he hits enter and leans back. Confused, he stares at the unseen screen for several moments.

Clearly bothered by what he sees, he cradles his head in his fingers as he considers something. Finally, he leans close to his computer and licks his lips, concentrating. Tearing away the top sheet of his betting notebook, he begins making notes.

Chapter Nine

It's a cloudless late afternoon, and the streets of central Reno have an old feel to them. Cutting between aging one-story homes and studded with junky and broken-down cars, the streets and their surroundings seem to have missed the boat for economic development. The pavement running the length of each road is disused and cracked, and most of the small businesses in the area are unique places, with "Palm Reader," "Private Massage," and various ethnic food stores being just a few examples of the challenging commercial environment.

Kalisa drives down one such street, frowning at addiction-addled homeless people and young wannabe tough guys who stroll through the area. Neither of these groups seem to mind showing themselves for who they are in the disadvantaged neighborhood, making the locality an unpleasant one.

Pulling to a curb beside a simple-but-functional home, Kalisa puts the car in park. She pivots to look at Seth, who sits in the front seat with a sad look. He doesn't say anything to Kalisa, but with his disappointed expression, he doesn't need to.

"OK, it's time to hang out with Daddy again," Kalisa says, trying to put on her best face. "You guys will have a great time; it'll be a guys' weekend."

Seth frowns, peering over at his mom doubtfully. "Mom, I'm tired of spending weekends with dad. When's he comin' home?"

Kalisa offers Seth a gloomy smile, not disagreeing with his depressed sentiments. Her gaze becomes distant, and her mind drifts to more enjoyable memories with her husband, to a time when everything seemed right in their world. For a few moments, those distant times when they were a team make her smile, and she can feel those past periods like they are part of the present world, part of her real present-day existence.

The thing about someone like her is that feelings and memories are not just transitory, they always percolate under the surface, ready to impose their distant emotions on the present. In the case of a long-forgotten moment of love that can be beneficial, but with the mass murder she experienced, the invoked feelings are usually unwelcome.

Coming back to the conscious present, Kalisa realizes her son is staring at her, looking with those innocent eyes for a mom that can connect in the present, just like Rick undoubtedly wished the same. Tousling Seth's hair, she stays quiet and motions to the waiting house with a

CHAPTER NINE

genuine smile. Swinging their creaky doors open, they silently exit the car.

While Seth waits, Kalisa collects his backpack and some bags of personal items from the trunk. Following him to the front door, Kalisa tries to sound cheerful. "OK, make sure to be a good boy and do everything your father says."

"Mom, I'm not six years old. Besides, Dad is a lot less strict than you."

Frowning at that morsel of information, Kalisa moves to knock at the door, but it swings open before she reaches it. Rick stares out, focusing down at Seth with an enormous grin.

Rick pointedly avoids making eye contact with Kalisa. "Hey buddy, you get bigger every time I see you. Are you like sixteen now, or what?"

"Dad, you say that every time…"

Smiling even broader, Rick interrupts and holds up two fingers, as if counting. "We got two things to do tonight. First, I got a new video game, and second, we'll get some pizza—that expensive stuff from Longlighters Pizza. Tonight is just between us, so you're worth every penny."

Seth smiles and looks up to Kalisa, all his bad thoughts pushed aside for the moment. Kalisa gives him a worried nod, realizing it's easier for Seth to deal with the separation than it is for her.

She holds out the bags, beckoning Rick to take them. "This is all his stuff for the weekend. And you can call at any time if you need…anything."

There's an awkward moment as all three realize the pause in Kalisa's voice could be interpreted as an offer of something decidedly cozier for the weekend—a fun time with all of them present. Seth is happy with the prospect, and he looks expectantly to his dad.

Rick isn't interested. After a moment passes, Rick shakes his head and takes the things from Kalisa's hands. He turns around and disappears inside, having avoided her gaze the entire time. Downcast, Seth waves goodbye and follows his dad in. The door clacks shut behind them without an audible goodbye.

Standing alone, Kalisa stares at the door. It takes her a while to come to terms with the rejection, and she realizes she must look pretty ridiculous staring at a door in this shitty area. After a deep breath, she turns back to the car, grinding her jaw and hating herself more every step of the way.

#

Kalisa sits in her car, staring down at the glowing screen of her phone. Outside, the area is dark, but the omnipresent lights of lampposts stretch all around her, spaced between all varieties of cars and trucks.

CHAPTER NINE

Kalisa looks at the mobile phone with a self-conscious grimace. She tentatively taps the virtual keys of her messenger program, and her expectant eyes shine a bit in the dim light of her front seat. Below, her text is to the point, almost pleading.

ARE YOU GUYS HAVING FUN?

On the screen, the same annoying checkmark shows that Rick has read the message, but her question still goes unanswered. It strikes Kalisa as infuriating that they designed the app this way, where someone can know their communication has been received, but also that the receiver doesn't give a shit about responding. It's typical for "progress" in the high-tech age, where it's so easy to exchange information with people, but everyone cares less and less about true interaction or politeness.

With a scowl, Kalisa puts the phone away and looks over the front seat. A recent fast-food meal and its wrappers are on the seat, along with a collection of plastic soda bottles. *I guess this is girl's night out, but you have to have real friends for that to work.*

Coming to a decision, Kalisa reaches across the front seat to the glovebox, where she rifles through some papers in search of something. Frustrated, she pulls out her phone and uses its light to pry through the rafts of old bills and car insurance paperwork.

Abruptly, she yanks out her prize: It's the envelope from her deceased grandfather, received just after his

DESPICABLE

death. She half-pulls the check out, staring at is zeros in the light from the outside streetlamp.

Gathering herself, she opens her car door and stands in the chilly night. Ahead of her is a well-lit casino, festooned with the neon regalia of its get-rich mental attraction. It's not her own workplace, because being a compulsive gambler is looked down upon by her bosses, and over the years she's found she likes to avoid gambling away from their prying eyes. She doubts there's a gambling addict in the world that enjoys losing in front of people that know and used to respect them.

Pacing towards the main entrance, she watches groups of twenty-somethings head into the main lobby. Their bright and hopeful eyes match her own desires for the night: a chance to live on the edge and finally hit the big jackpot—to be a big winner, for once in her pathetic life.

Stopping under the main entrance, all manner of diverse folks enter and exit ahead of Kalisa, oblivious to her internal war for self-control. Standing rigid, she struggles with manic thoughts and dreams, while knowing exactly where this rodeo is headed: to the self-imposed land of personal poverty. *Ahh, fuck it anyway—just one last time. Just once, I gotta win.*

With a deep breath, she collects her strength and walks into the opulent building, once again letting the pull of instant gratification overwhelm her otherwise rational mind.

CHAPTER NINE

#

Inside, Kalisa stands at a crowded roulette table. Surrounded by half-inebriated and wildly gesticulating gamblers, her eyes are alive as she pans them around the table. While arms from fellow players grab chips and point at particular spots, she holds back her own money, avoiding committing herself as the roulette ball spins in a lazy circle. As the crowd waits in anticipatory silence, she watches the ball, trying to gauge its place and potential landing spot.

Reaching forward, Kalisa quickly pushes the whole of her piled wealth on a single bet, the "2nd 12" numbers of the roulette board. She just manages to beat the deadline for placing wagers.

"No more bets," says the croupier, and he sweeps the waiting group with an indifferent frown and a forbidding hand, just as the ball pings and bounces for a long and torturous moment. "Black seventeen."

The crowd erupts in raucous applause, and Kalisa pumps her arm in triumph. She takes time hugging the strangers around her, smiling a winner's smile while a huge stack of fresh chips is pushed next to her.

Later, Kalisa sits at a huge bank of slot machines, and along with the clicking and beeping that accompanies wheels on the huge LCD screens, a two million dollar "Grand Prize" is offered for a perfect combination of flashing diamonds.

DESPICABLE

Depressed, Kalisa watches the screen with anguished eyes. She raises a lip in disgust, shaking her head at her bad luck and hoping for a comeback. After a couple of more spins, she lowers her eyes and runs her sweaty hands through her hair, wanting to pull it out by the roots.

Leaning at a cozy house bar, Kalisa stands while playing a video poker game at the end of a line of machines. Moving quickly, she slaps at the buttons, chasing the Royal Flush across multiple played hands—but having little luck. Around her, the area is silent, with only the distant beat of pop music offering entertainment to break the mood.

Frustrated, Kalisa takes a shot of vodka with a grimace, then points to the bartender for another. The confused man shakes his head in response, gesturing to a line of several other alcoholic drinks already awaiting her attention.

Kalisa sighs and finally sits at the machine. She continues smacking at the buttons, hoping that slapping the plastic knobs harder will bring a more beneficial result.

Pissed off, Kalisa stretches her arms towards the ceiling in a stretch. When she drops her hands back down, she notices the time on her watch: 3:30 AM. She scowls, trying to concentrate through her booze-induced buzz.

At a blackjack table, Kalisa has a huge pile of ships stacked in front of her, grinning like a contented

- 134 -

CHAPTER NINE

schoolboy. Strangers stand behind her, egging her on and shouting as the dealer flips a winning hand in her favor.

"Blackjack—winner is paid 3-to-2...again," says the bespectacled dealer, and his tone says even he doesn't believe her luck. As he moves more chips in front of Kalisa, her eyes brighten at the colored rows of pink pieces with "$1000" stenciled on their surface.

Steeling herself, Kalisa looks again at her watch. The only other player at the table, a chubby old man, stands and saunters from the game, searching elsewhere for his fortune.

Now by herself, Kalisa inhales deeply, thinking over her next move. She takes a swig of beer from a lukewarm bottle, pondering the possibilities of the moment as she swishes the cheap suds in her mouth.

Coming to a decision, Kalisa figures the time is now or never. Whatever the result, her best chance to make a change in her sad life centers on one flip of the cards. One final foray into that strange concept known as luck. Any statistics course will tell you that such a thing doesn't exist, but when it's all on the line, luck is really all that matters.

Kalisa pushes every chip she has into the betting circle, and a score of spectators focus on her like she's lost her mind. The dealer is also surprised, but he recovers and smirks with an *it's-your-funeral* expression. As he arranges the pile of chips for the camera above to know the stakes, the dealer trades a worried glance with a nearby pit boss.

Looking around, Kalisa acknowledges the craziness of her bet with a nod towards the suddenly quiet onlookers. "Well, you only live once, right?"

Murmurs of worry from the crowd are the only answers to her question, and Kalisa isn't reassured with the evolving game or her choice to lay it all on the line. It's kind of like this with life itself—taking risks—but at least with the cards or dice, a failed result won't mean your family is hacked to death and stacked like cordwood in your hometown's main street. Scrimping to pay the bills is mild in comparison to that ever-present memory in Kalisa's tortured mind. *Let's get on with it, then.*

Kalisa motions for the man to deal, and the entire area goes quiet when cards are snapped out of the chute and flipped in front of her. Looking at her two cards, she takes in her count of nineteen—an ace and an eight. It's a good hand, but far from indestructible.

From Kalisa's study of various card counting systems, she knows it will win a majority of the time, but she's aware a majority matters little when everything rides on one hand. It's like saying you have a fifty-five percent chance of surviving an operation, only to realize the price for being on the bad side of those odds is a date with a mortician.

Kalisa peers up, and the dealer reveals his up-card—a ten of spades. Nodding at her cards, she waves her hand

CHAPTER NINE

to indicate she'll stay on her dealt hand. In response, the dealer flips his own unseen hole card.

Kalisa's eyes go wide in shock, processing what lies before her.

#

The coffee shop is largely unoccupied at this time in the morning. Clean tables are arranged in comfortable rows, and only a few denizens of late-night gambling have summoned the courage to have a meal at such an hour.

Kalisa is one of those hardy souls, and she sits at a cushy booth in the corner of the establishment. She looks down at her phone, tapping at the screen with relaxed pokes of her fingertips. A cup of coffee with a collection of empty sweetener packets lie on the table, evidence of her caffeine addiction.

"Haven't seen you this early in a while," says Barb, a waitress in her fifties with red hair and a reassuring grin. She stands above Kalisa, a coffee carafe held in her hand. With her working-class bearing and amicable appearance, she looks like she stepped whole from a 1980s diner sitcom.

Kalisa smiles up at Barb, giving her a considered and kind smile. Her eyes are puffy from crying, but she's calm and controlled in the mellow morning, apparently avoiding a hangover from the night's drinking. "I swore I would stay away. It worked, too. For a while, at least..."

DESPICABLE

Giving her best motherly impression, Barb sits in the seat opposite Kalisa. "It never works forever, darlin'. Been watching it my whole life, and they…you…always come back."

Kalisa is surprised by the waitress taking a seat, but she's happy for the company. She nods in response, admitting the truth to Barb's statement by staying quiet.

Barb continues. "How did you do? Did you at least win a little? The best way to play the casinos is to walk at least some of the time when you're ahead; that way, it isn't always a crushing loss to your pocketbook. My mom was able to play most of her life by following that strategy, staying in the game in the long run. Most people gotta move from the area if they play too much—it's too expensive to keep up."

Kalisa takes in the advice, realizing everything she said is true. Unfortunately, she's never been good at leaving while she's ahead—at least most of the time.

Kalisa lowers her gaze and speaks slowly, like every word clearing her lips is painfully considered and utterly true. "Last night was the last night I will ever gamble, as long as I live. I can say that with all certainty—no bullshit."

"I hope that that's true," replies Barb, but she doesn't bother hiding her doubt about the promise. "It'd be nice to live without that monkey on your back."

"Yeah, it will, Barb. Now, for once in my life I can work on what's important, not just fun in the moment.

CHAPTER NINE

Every day that goes by, I can see everything clearer, like my eyes were blinded before."

Barb peers at Kalisa, mulling over her seemingly serious commitment to overcoming her weakness. A look of respect crosses her face, and she reaches out to top off Kalisa's coffee with a new splash of the casino's best brew. Standing, Barb pats Kalisa on the shoulder and walks toward the kitchen, her role of sage confessor again fulfilled.

Smiling faintly, Kalisa tears open another packet of sugar and pours it into her cup. As she stirs the contents, a hopeful smile remains locked over her sleep-deprived features.

Chapter Ten

The kitchen is full of bowls and packages of food, with flour, pudding, and every ingredient known to man or woman scattered across the counter. Staring down at the items, Kalisa nods in quiet satisfaction.

Glancing over to the kitchen table, Kalisa grins at a massive cake perched on a plastic cake holder. Swathed in chocolate frosting, it has enough icing to kill an army of diabetics.

Catching herself at forgetting something, Kalisa moves to the oven and bends to look into its crusted interior. A tray of perfectly browned rolls is done baking in the dim light, just visible through the old and foggy oven window. Putting on oven mitts, she pulls the tray out and sets it on the last clear space of countertop.

Removing her protective gloves, Kalisa watches over the kitchen like a conquering general. Everything is perfect, with the baked goodies in perfect symmetry of taste and timing. Glancing at her watch, she begins collecting the food into bags, hurrying around the tight confines of the messy area. Her planning schedule is tight, and she wants this to be perfect.

A sharp rap on the door interrupts her preparations, and she casts a confused glare at the cheap door. *Nobody ever visits me.*

Kalisa yanks a sharp knife from a brace of cutlery on the counter. She approaches the door with a worried frown.

As she gets near the door, the voice of Eddie's mom, Irina, comes from the other side. She is clearly distraught, and panic bleeds into her words. "Kalisa, have you seen Eddie?"

Surprised, Kalisa sets her improvised weapon aside and pulls the door open. A woman in her late forties stands there, backlit by the afternoon sun. Running mascara covers much of her face, and her terrified eyes meet Kalisa's.

Mortified, Kalisa tilts her head in confusion and motions Irina into the apartment. As the disheveled woman drops into one of the kitchen chairs, Kalisa tries keeping her voice low, hoping to calm her down. "Eddie? I saw him the other day. He helped me with an errand…"

Kalisa leaves out the rest of the story from Irina. First, she's not sure it would be a good idea to let her know about Kalisa's paranoia, and second, she isn't certain Irina will not blame her…for whatever's going on.

"He called me two nights ago," says Irina, trying to hold back more tears. "He said he was going for a job

CHAPTER TEN

interview. Now, he's not answering his phone. I have a really bad feeling…all the way into my stomach, like there's something really wrong."

Perplexed, Kalisa shakes her head, not knowing what to say. She tries a bullshit explanation anyway. "I'm sure he's just somewhere with his friends. You know kids, always thinking only about themselves."

Kalisa walks to the kitchen and opens the fridge. Extracting a carton of orange juice, she pours a glass and collects a piping hot roll for Irina on the way back to the table. She gingerly places them in front of the agitated mother. Irina ignores the offering.

"I called the police," says Irina, and she shakes with fear as she tries to control her anxiety, "but because of his past…problems, they think he's a runaway. I know he would never leave without telling me. He's a good boy; he never hurt anyone in his life. Where could he be?"

After a pause, Irina breaks down in tears, crying in great sobs, like only a desperate mother of missing offspring could do. It's a tone of trauma and mourning Kalisa knows all too well.

Kalisa places a concerned hand on Irina's shoulder, offering support to the hysterical woman. While patting her gently on the back, however, a more informed worry tugs at Kalisa's face, along with a hint of guilt. *What the fuck is going on?*

#

DESPICABLE

The gas station has only one car at this time of day, and Kalisa finds herself pumping gas at the outside island of the expansive facility. A convenience store stands some distance away, and it holds only a few customer vehicles in its parking lot.

Trying to ignore the toxic fumes, Kalisa finishes pumping the pungent fuel in her clunky car, topping it off with several squeezes. Even as she crams every last bit of fuel in the tank, she knows there's really no reason to do so. It's not like the extra splash of gasoline will help her avoid running out of fuel, but nobody ever said human beings are fully rational.

Replacing the gas cap and pump, Kalisa pulls her receipt from the dispenser. Frowning at the cost, she wonders why people spend so much of their working hours financing this outrageous cost. She has heard people all over the world live within walking distance to their job, but for some reason, Americans are stuck driving twenty or thirty miles to work—each way. She would also like to see one time in her life when she could finally be surprised by how cheap something is, as opposed to always being shocked by how fast the cost increases.

On her way to the driver's seat, she stops for a moment, noticing her reflection in the car window. She's a little taken aback at her image, with dark circles under the eyes of what should still be a young woman. Thinking

CHAPTER TEN

for a second, she runs her hand through her hair, as if doing so might make her a little more attractive for Rick.

Kalisa catches her breath, realizing Rick might never again give a shit what she looks like. Giving up on the finger comb, she stares at herself for just a bit longer, hoping to have kept a little bit of that beauty that Rick once treasured.

In the reflection, she sees a police car pull in front of her vehicle, blocking her from leaving. Turning and walking to the cop car, her gaze falls on Lance, who sits comfortably in the driver's seat. He has expensive sunglasses, and his self-important sense of stud-mania radiates through the window. *What the fuck was I thinking? He looks like the King of Cool—for fourteen-year-olds.*

Lance thumbs the window down with an electric whir and focuses up at Kalisa. "Hi, Kalisa, how are you?"

Kalisa nods in response, letting her tone sound suspicious. "Lance, are you following me?"

"Not hardly," Lance replies, and he holds up a sheet of paper with extensive writing on it. "You're the one who forced me to get this."

Lance lowers his voice and looks around, apparently convinced a ghost somewhere near the deserted gas pumps will hear him. "And it wasn't easy; I had to call in a few favors."

Kalisa reaches for the paper, not bashful about wanting the data. Lance holds it just out her reach and dangles it in the air. He removes his sunglasses for dramatic effect as he meets her gaze. "Listen to me, Kalisa. I'm sorry about what I did, what *WE* did. It was wrong and selfish, and it won't happen again. I...never meant to..."

As his voice trails off, Kalisa tilts her head in response, taking a measure of his feelings—whether they're real or imagined. She doesn't respond directly but allows her skeptical stare to offer a direct answer: *You can be certain of that, big boy.*

"But don't try this again," Lance continues. "You can certainly make my life miserable—and probably get me fired. But blackmail is a crime, and you're going down with me if it happens again."

Lance gestures to the still-present wedding band she wears, and Kalisa protectively places her other hand over the expensive ring. "And I'm not the only one who should want the past to remain hidden."

Kalisa is impressed with Lance's chutzpah, and she stares down with a newfound respect for the serial womanizer. One thing is true over all times and cultures: it takes balls to take a risk, but it takes brains to know when to quit.

Kalisa snatches the paper from Lance's hand before he can pull it back again. Staring at her former lover, she nods in agreement.

#

CHAPTER TEN

Holding her large cake box and a plastic bag full of rolls, Kalisa nudges her car door shut. As she struggles nimbly toward Rick's house, she looks a bit like an ant dragging a ponderous morsel across the dirt near a recent picnic.

Getting to the front door, it's pushed open before she can knock, and Seth's grinning face greets her at the threshold. He claps his hands together while leering at the treats she carries. "Hi, mom. You got cake. Can we have some now? Please?"

Kalisa smiles at her son, gesturing further into the house with her full arms. "These are for your father, but if it's OK with him, you get a big gooey slice of chocolate."

Ecstatic, the boy turns and runs into the home. Kalisa frowns at the lack of his help and gently makes her way into the front room, banging her culinary baggage on the way in.

The inside of Rick's house is tidy, if somewhat empty of decoration or domestic splendor. In the front room, a cheap couch is arranged in front of an LCD TV hooked to a gaming console. There are no decorations on the faded walls, announcing the place as a bachelor pad par excellence.

Rick emerges from the hallway, dressed for comfort in baggy sweatpants and a loose shirt. Unshaven, he looks the part of a carefree single man. "You're like two hours early. Something wrong?"

DESPICABLE

Kalisa continues holding her baked goods. She tilts her head in frustration. "Nothing wrong, except you aren't answering my texts."

Rick raises an eyebrow, surprised at her forwardness. His demeanor is cool and distant. "Wasn't aware I had to."

Kalisa nods, conceding his point. Trying out a pleasant smile, she holds out the cake. "I made your favorite cake and rolls. Thought maybe you'd like some home cooking. Pizza and burgers get a little old, right?"

Rick focuses on Kalisa, but his thoughts are hidden as he considers the offer. Her muscles get weary as she mentally begs for him to take the damn food.

Rick gestures to the coffee table. "Set them there, if you would. We were just playing some video games, killing zombies in a father-and-son tandem."

Kalisa unloads her packages, smothering the table. Stepping back, she takes a deep breath and faces Rick. She avoids trying to smile, knowing he'll see through any more ass-kissing. "I came to talk—if you're willing."

"Then talk…but I'm not sure what else there is to say."

Walking to the entrance of the kitchen, Kalisa pokes her head in the other room. Seth sits there, munching from a bowl of Fruit Loops and reading a comic book. Seeing him occupied, she turns back to Rick and keeps her tone low. 'Rick, there's no excuse for what I did…to you or our family. I know this."

CHAPTER TEN

"Do ya think? That must have taken a lot of brainstorming."

There's a pause as Rick collects himself and shakes his head to clear away his emotional nightmare. Stepping back from Kalisa, he runs his hands through his hair and stares at the ceiling, trying to control himself. "What did I ever do to you to jump into some dude's bed? It isn't bad enough you spend half our money at those fucking casinos? Now you gotta make a fool out of me? What's next, Kalisa? You wanna beat me in the town square?"

"I know I've been a rotten person—,"

"You don't know shit," Rick interrupts. "You do whatever you want…to chase away those demons in your fucked-up brain. Everyone else gets to pay for your shitty past."

Ricks points to the kitchen and is just able to keep his voice quiet. "You think it's fair he gets to play *Musical Chairs* with his parents, just because you had to do whatever you wanted?"

Kalisa shakes her head, her eyes growing watery. She doesn't know what to say, and she stutters out a defense. 'I…should have…gotten help sooner."

"At least we agree on that, I should have got a brain scan for being stupid enough to marry you," Rick says, and he stares intently at Kalisa, jaw clenched and eyes wounded. "You fucking broke my heart, and now…I don't know what to do."

Kalisa is torn by the image. She reaches out to him, trying to offer comfort. Rick bats away her hand and steps around her.

Wiping his own eyes, Rick raises his voice. "Buddy, you and mom are going home early today. Get your stuff together, OK?"

Looking back to Kalisa, Rick recovers, burying his emotions under a cold stare. "Thanks for the food. Go ahead and let yourself out when he's ready to go."

Without another word, he walks down the hallway, disappearing into his room with a gentle click of the door behind him.

#

The day has become overcast and drizzly, with a pervasive mist hanging over the residential area. A number of assorted pedestrians walk through the working-class neighborhood, huddling against chilly weather and pulling their coats tight.

Kalisa strides through the brisk weather, her eyes focused on a dilapidated housing complex straight ahead. She doesn't appear concerned with the uncomfortable temperature or the unpleasant climate, even as a cold wind picks up and drives the water into her scrunched-up face.

Kalisa approaches a door on the ground floor of a shoddy building, one that has rows of identical entrances

CHAPTER TEN

facing the street. Each of the doors is painted a dirty brown, and the building's siding has red-chipped paint, screaming for proper maintenance.

Approaching door 4, Kalisa stops. She grimaces as she considers her options, ignoring the sheen of water that coats her face. Inhaling a deep breath, she gently knocks on the worn wood.

After a moment, the door swings inwards, and her father's face squints into the cold air. Dressed in a comfortable robe, he pushes his horn-rimmed glasses further up his weathered nose. His features catch in surprise as he peers at Kalisa, wondering what's wrong and not liking what he sees. "Daughter, what brings you here today? You haven't visited in years."

"It's been one year, dad," replies Kalisa. The collection of beaded water on her features gives her a careless and unkempt appearance, one that is worryingly uncaring of her surroundings.

Martin doesn't respond to her correction. Part of laying a guilt trip on a child, even an adult one, means not worrying if they're offended you got the date wrong for the time passed since a last visit.

Kalisa leans closer to Martin, keeping her voice steady but sounding lonely and destitute. "I need to talk to you. I got nowhere else to go…everything is…wrong."

Abruptly, Kalisa leans entirely into her dad, clutching onto him like a lost schoolgirl. She begins sobbing as she

DESPICABLE

buries her head into his fluffy robe, her tears mixing with the dew from the moist air.

Surprised, Martin stands for a time, not knowing how to respond. Slowly, he raises his arms and embraces her in a consoling hug.

For some time they stand there, not a word passing between them.

Chapter Eleven

Martin leans over the stove, sniffing the air above a pan full of sizzling sausages. To the side are other crackling skillets with scrambled eggs and hash browns, making for a raucous and aromatic kitchen area.

Gathering two plates, Martin scoops prodigious helpings of the steaming food onto each. As he balances the stack of breakfast goodness, he moves to a kitchen table, where Kalisa waits with hungry eyes. She licks her lips as he slides the comfort meal in front of her.

"Eat, daughter," says Martin. "No purpose was ever served by starving oneself."

The kitchen and apartment around them is a cozy and clean area, with sturdy furniture and a homey environment. Photos on the walls show Kalisa and the rest of the family from long ago, with her smiling brother and mom occupying prominent places within several clean picture frames.

Kalisa stares at one photo on the wall near the table, where her mom and brother are posed near a horse. Both

DESPICABLE

are smiling, and they stand on a farm with rows of crops in the background. Their grins are infectious, causing Kalisa a smile, even across all the time and tragedy that's passed since that distant place in her life.

Kalisa drops her gaze, her smile fading as she returns to the present. She scoops a mouthful of fluffy eggs in her mouth and fixes Martin with an appreciative nod at the delicious taste.

"So, you now have two missing people that you know?" asks Martin, his face full of fatherly worry. "Life is full of coincidences."

"Yeah, but disappearing in the middle of the city, with no trace? Within the same week? That's more than unlikely; it's completely bizarre."

Martin nods thoughtfully. "Yes, that is unusual. But what could it be but a random chance of nature?"

Kalisa sets down her fork, looking deeper into Martin's words than he imagined. "I think it could be nature, yes. Regular people missing in the middle of a city isn't normal. I also know I've been followed lately."

"You've said this, daughter. But what proof do you have? If you want to be taken seriously in this country, you cannot sound like a conspiracy theorist."

Kalisa reaches inside her sweater, extracting a folded paper and smoothing it out carefully. She places the rumpled sheet in front of her father, who looks skeptically at it.

"What is this?" Martin asks.

CHAPTER ELEVEN

"This is the address registered to two cars that were following me," replies Kalisa. "The boy who's missing took photos of their plates. And…my ex-lover cop ran the plates for me when I blackmailed him to do it."

Martin's eyes go wide for a disbelieving moment, but his gaze shifts to vague interest as he focuses on the paper. Looking out the window, Kalisa avoids saying more, torn between deep shame at her actions and the need to talk about it with someone.

Martin speaks low, a dark smile chasing away his scowl. "Then something good came out of your stupidity. I hope you learned your lesson, because only through mistakes can we access God's redemption."

Catching himself, Martin stops short of his lecture and looks down again at the sheet of information. He traces his finger over the scribbled name and address, growing alarmed. "Mathias Baudin? From the funeral home? Why would he be following you? What possible reason…?"

Kalisa shakes her head, equally perplexed. "I wish I knew. Dude was creepy as hell, but that's kinda to be expected. Guys that handle dead people for a living aren't on my list of everyday normal folks."

Pursing his lips, Martin concentrates on his daughter, working through the weird events. Nodding, he pushes away his food, his breakfast abandoned. He stands and looks down at Kalisa as he considers what comes next. "We will go there, today, and have a talk with Mr. Baudin.

We'll ask him exactly what interest he has in my daughter."

Kalisa is relieved at the sight of her father's concern, even though she's worried about a proposed visit to the funeral home. Life is bad enough to make it through conflicts alone, and having family to help in such a strange circumstance makes her feel relieved. A smile crosses her lips and a sense of pride works its way into her chest, replacing the ache of sorrow and angst.

Martin walks to the kitchen, where he reaches to a cabinet above the refrigerator. Pulling a holster free from behind a flour bag, he extracts a revolver from the aged and wrapped leather. Expertly, he withdraws the weapon and snaps the cylinder open, checking the condition of the shiny cartridges inside. "And Mr. Baudin is going to give us some answers."

#

Kalisa peers through her smudged windshield, squinting through the sun-glinted glass. "It doesn't look like anyone's there. You sure they're open today?"

Martin answers with a scowl, one he seems to have perfected over the years. He gestures to the back of the funeral business, where several cars are parked at varied angles. "Someone is there. Do you recognize any of those cars?"

CHAPTER ELEVEN

The weather around them is chilly and forbidding, and clouds blot out most of the light in the late afternoon. A faint howl from Reno's ever-present wind leaks into the car's interior.

Kalisa shakes her head at the vehicles, which are an assortment of domestic sedans and SUVs—no expensive European cars among them.

Nodding to the front of the death-house, Martin climbs out of the car. As he rights himself, he adjusts his holster under a puffy orange coat. The outerwear went out of style with the last episode of *Knight Rider*, but it somehow seems appropriate to Martin's elderly and unthreatening appearance.

Inside the vehicle, Kalisa checks the chamber of a small nine-millimeter pistol and tucks it into a shoulder holster. She's never had the need for guns, but it's far smarter to have it when you don't need it than the reverse. She never could figure out why folks in the movies never carried weapons when they needed them, especially when everyone watching the damn thing knew bad guys were soon to visit the storyline. Her story is yet to be determined, but she sure as hell won't be unprepared for whatever's coming. She went through that once, and the result was less than satisfactory.

Clambering out next to her father, she zips up her own faded jacket and faces the suddenly imposing building. After a quick glance at each other, they make their way to the front entrance.

Leaning forward, Martin is almost surprised when the cold metal door handle opens, and light from the outside floods into the calm interior. As they walk gingerly inside, they notice that nothing has changed from the decorations and ornamentation, as the mellow reception area has reverted to its former status as a reception room after the celebration they had a few days ago.

The room is without any workers or mourners, with the constant hum of funereal music being the only thing to greet them. Kalisa understands the sad tones are meant to offer a peaceful backdrop to the place, but in truth, she's really getting sick of it. In fact, if there is a hell, it must include having to listen to corpse music for an eternity, with no respite or end to the droll sounds. For once, Kalisa would like to hear Judas Priest or perhaps Def Leppard in such an establishment. Hell, even the occasional ballad of Yanni would break things up a bit.

"Mr. Baudin, this is Martin Kinigi," Martin says, his voice filling the empty place. "I should like to speak to you. Immediately."

No person or sound answers him, and Martin looks to his daughter with a frown. Kalisa shrugs, moving her gaze around and offering her own gloomy consideration of the place.

After more moments of silence, Martin motions to a door at the back of the room, one that they hadn't seen used in their prior visits. This time it's Kalisa that tries the

CHAPTER ELEVEN

door handle, and she is also surprised when it opens easily.

A hallway stretches before them, but the carpet from the other room doesn't follow the lighted path forward; instead, white tiles line the floor. At the end of the hall is a double metal door, like the type from a hospital that allows people or things to be pushed through them.

To the left of those doors is a freezer-like doorway with a latching metal entrance and darkness beyond its fogged window.

After walking carefully to the swinging doors, Martin gestures beyond it, where lights bleed around its edges. Kalisa shrugs in answer, preferring a place that at least has illumination to the cold freezer door to the side.

Martin eases the door open, and inside is revealed a large antiseptic room. Four metal tables with draining plugs at their end are lined up in a row, spaced in the middle.

The walls are empty and white, with only diagrams of the human body to break up the monotony. Kalisa realizes this must be the preparation area for the dead, and she wrinkles her nose at her father. Martin doesn't appear bothered by its purpose and moves to one of the tables.

The shiny metal of the corpse-preparation tables are clean and wiped down with disinfectant. Moving close to one, Kalisa keeps her disgusted look as her gaze moves from the shiny metal to a tray of various tools to the side.

DESPICABLE

From what looks like a bone saw to several sharp instruments and an array of thick scissors, she knows this isn't a job she'll be applying for any time soon. She also realizes no cleaning solution on earth can sterilize the muck that these tables and tools see on a daily basis.

The creak of a metal cabinet door being opened gets Kalisa's attention away from the table. She moves next to Martin, who has just opened the massive metal cabinet door against the wall of the room.

Peering inside, Kalisa and Martin see a huge collection of glass containers lined up across multiple shelves. Some are unmarked, but others have chemical-sounding names written on stickers. It's unclear what each solution or chemical is used for, but it appears every noxious substance known to humanity is represented in the assortment.

Bending down to the bottom shelf, a large container—it's almost a crystal pitcher, like the type used to pour expensive wine—catches Kalisa's eye. Inside the container is a green jelly-like substance, and it seems to glow, almost pulsing with its catchy and sparkling hue.

Kalisa motions to it, inclining her head to Martin and whispering. "You ever seen something like this?"

Her father shakes his head, an intrigued look on his wrinkled features.

Kalisa reaches in and grabs the pitcher, pulling it closer to the edge for closer inspection. She furrows her brow as she uncaps the top. A strange and unrecognizable

CHAPTER ELEVEN

odor wafts up from inside the canter, causing Kalisa to nearly retch. It's a combination of a sweet smell, almost like an odd form of paprika, with a distant tinge of death, like an exposed animal carcass left to rot in the sun. She steps away from the cabinet as she tries to avoid getting sick.

Unafraid, Martin lowers himself to the shelf, grunting from the effort of the squat. Taking out a handkerchief, he collects some of the bizarre substance from the bottle's rim and folds it into his pocket. Moving carefully, he re-stops the container and eases the cabinet shut.

Standing, Martin refocuses on the door they entered, motioning that they should go. When they exit the preparation room towards the reception room, however, Kalisa stops in front of the freezer door. Even as Martin shakes his head at the idea, Kalisa nods her head to the cold door.

Grasping the handle, Kalisa opens the freezer door with surprising ease, like it was made for easy access. Martin frowns at her actions and focuses on the darkness beyond.

As they step inside, the lights go on automatically, illuminating a large freezer. However, instead of human remains on tables or in lockers, rows and rows of meat are perched on hooks, like it's a butcher's warehouse.

Except, the meat is not normal; it is of horrible quality, and it's not immediately obvious from which animal it's hacked from. Clumps of dark fur stick from the patches of hanging gray flesh.

Walking a few steps into the rows of atrocious animal tissue, Kalisa's breath plumes out in misty condensation. She reaches up, extending her fingers to touch a rack of meat, fascinated by its vile condition. Just as her fingers get close to the putrid exterior, Martin grabs her hand.

"It might not be safe, daughter," whispers Martin. "And in any case, I do not wish to be here any longer. This place is…not as it seems, or even should be."

Kalisa doesn't disagree. "What the hell is this? What do they need this nasty meat for?"

Martin doesn't answer, his worried features showing he has no idea.

Nodding to the freezer's entrance, Kalisa moves to retrace their steps and get out of this crazy place. She doesn't know why rotting animal meat would be in a funeral home, and she doesn't want to stay longer to find out.

Shutting the freezer, they walk towards the reception area, quickening their pace as they go. Pushing the door open, they emerge from the tile hallway into the well-lit reception space. Not hesitating, they angle towards the front door and a quick escape.

"To what do I owe this visit of father and daughter," asks Mathias Baudin, and he steps from a recessed alcove near the viewing room. He wears an expensive tailored

CHAPTER ELEVEN

suit, and his hands are clasped comfortably in front of himself. He grins the smile of a self-assured predator.

Spinning around, Kalisa and Martin are surprised. Martin's hand moves to the grip of his revolver, while Kalisa's hovers near her own weapon.

Mathias looks amused as he notices their *fight or flight* demeanors. Not a hint of worry colors his relaxed expression. "Please, friends. Let us not resort to violence; that's rarely the best path of choice in this short life we lead. I fear you would not like the results of such actions, in any case."

Kalisa is the first to respond. She takes a step toward the business owner, surprising everyone, including herself. "Who are you, Baudin? And none of this bullshit about your owning this…business."

"I'm certainly a businessman, amongst other things," replies Baudin, and his grin broadens as he takes a step towards Kalisa. "I'm just wondering what brings two of my clients to see me today."

Martin keeps his hand on the butt of his revolver, raising his tone in an aggressive huff. "You are having my daughter followed, and if that is true, you are no friend of ours."

Mathias raises an eyebrow, turning toward Martin with an impressed stare. "Ahh, so that was you that looked us up? Very impressive, and not so easy to do."

"It was me, Baudin, and your surveillance was shit," Kalisa says, pointing to herself. "A child could've noticed it. And what's with the expensive cars?"

Mathias chuckles, and his attention returns to Kalisa. "The world is not always about you, Kalisa, and in any case, we are free to go where we wish in public, correct?"

"Who is this 'we' you are talking about, Baudin?" asks Kalisa.

"Yes, I would like that answer as well," Martin chimes in, and he moves protectively close to his daughter's side.

Mathias ignores their questions, instead walking over to a coffee table stacked with refreshments. He thinks for several quiet moments, mulling something over before adopting a professorial tone. "I will offer you one truth and a bit of advice from your visit today…before you leave."

Pulling a clean glass from a nearby cupboard, Mathias pops two pieces of ice in it from a container. Moving carefully, he splashes a generous dose of whiskey over the cubes. Holding up the glass, he savors the smell, drawing in the unique odor of the aged liquid.

After taking a sip, he speaks with an amicable voice. "First, a truth: you have nothing to fear from me or anyone in my employ. I am not your enemy, and I would prefer for it to remain that way."

Taking another drink, Mathias walks to the far wall, where a beautiful painting of the African Savannah hangs. On its canvass is a host of animals, from gazelles to lions

CHAPTER ELEVEN

and some distant giraffes. Kalisa is surprised she didn't notice the painting earlier; it's beautiful, lifelike, and likely very expensive.

Mathias continues. "In Africa, there's a fierce predator: the hyena. It is actually a scavenger, but it spends a lifetime feeding off the kills of others. It finds strength in its large groups."

Mathias walks over to the alcove where he stood earlier. He reaches into a vase and extracts a flower, one with many-colored petals protruding from it. "And the hyena's group and its own fierceness protect it from a world of enemies. In many ways, it is the king of all its surveys."

Mathias begins plucking petals from the flower. He palms all the petals, until only a single white one remains on the stem. "Unless…it sometimes ventures too far after what it wants—near a lion's pride, for example. Now, it may see what it wants…and even try to get it."

Mathias sets the single-petal stem on a table. Looking at his guests, he smiles again. "And find that it is cut off—doomed—because it did not accept that there are boundaries that should never be crossed."

Mathias gently smashes the remainder of the petals, crushing them in his palms. His smile wilts, and his face becomes fierce and serious. He opens his hands, brushing the plant's debris on the spotless floor. "Remember that, both of you, for your own happiness. The world is a far more dangerous place than even you could know."

Entranced with the story, Kalisa stares openly at Mathias, wondering what to say or how to respond. His bearing and stature seem to have grown, and she can feel his charisma radiating through the room. Not knowing what to do, she looks to her father.

Martin is also affected by the exchange, and they take turns gulping and looking at Mathias. Neither of them move, as if they're waiting for permission to leave.

Returning their gaze, Mathias' grin returns, and his bright white teeth seem to take up half of his mouth. He nods toward the front entrance, graciously bidding the Kinigis goodbye.

Relieved, Kalisa and Martin hurry outside into the fading light of day.

#

It is night, and inside the car, Lance stares down at a hand-held computer game. The brightly lit miniature display illuminates his features in the darkness, and his face is puckered in concentration. He tilts the game left and right, as if steering something within the device.

On the screen below, his character is fighting from a first-person perspective, holding up a pistol and blasting away at hordes of incoming zombies. Their devilish maws, putrid faces, and otherworldly moans pursue him through a graveyard, where he spins about, looking for an exit from his imminent death.

CHAPTER ELEVEN

He is quickly overcome, with the shambling hordes dragging him down as he tries to reload. As the undead moaning increases, the blood-red lettering of "Game Over, You Lose" is painted across the mobile display.

"Shit," shouts Lance, and he throws the controller on the patrol car's front seat in a fit of rage. It's the sort of rage that often accompanies computer-generated death, but Lance has had a whole lifetime to sharpen that anger. He doesn't understand why he's never been good at computer games, which is in itself not a problem; no, the problem is he loves playing, and while he spends much of his time fighting people online throughout the world, he usually gets crushed by teens and children alike.

Lance sighs aloud, thinking it's not fair to love to do something and yet be horrible at it. At least he's not a painter or a writer, because in those circumstances the whole world gets to witness your awfulness, even if you're enjoying yourself. At least with gaming, he can be anonymous while he sucks.

Outside his car, the night is clear. Under the strong moon's light, scrub brush and sparse foliage are visible in the high-desert landscape. His police cruiser faces a lonely highway, and the cracked blacktop runs through a desolate and uninhabited area, creating an isolated feeling.

Shaking away his feelings of game inadequacy, Lance climbs out of the car. The elevated plateau of the Nevada terrain stretches far into the distance, where mountains and elevated hills hover at the edge of the skyline. It's certainly beautiful in its own way, but it's also a bit creepy. Lance can imagine settlers plodding across the area in wagons a hundred and fifty years ago, watching the never-ending skies and struggling through dangerous ravines and horrible weather.

He shakes his head, glad for the good fortune of not being born in such a time. *Fuck that.*

Reaching into his front pocket, Lance withdraws his smokes. His one guilty pleasure is smoking, the one bad thing he allows himself from time-to-time. He works out like a fanatic, makes bank at a job that mostly allows him to do his own thing, and has an assortment of girlfriends, but for some reason, he needs at least a half-dozen cancer sticks per day to truly feel better. He lights one of the cigarettes, inhaling the wonderful toxins with a guilty shrug.

Speaking of girlfriends, he's having a hard time getting over this latest episode with Kalisa. There's just something about her that makes his mind replay their time together, a certain carefree way she lives in the moment. It's exciting and…sexy.

He's got plenty of other women to occupy his time, but there's nothing that'll quite replace her. Besides, she's the only black girl he's ever dated, so where's he gonna get that flavor of affection in the future? He's heard about both guys and girls getting the "jungle fever," and with a chuckle, he realizes he might have to change tactics in the

CHAPTER ELEVEN

future. *Not many black girls are interested in white cops, but there's got to be a few, right?*

In the distance, Lance sees the emerging lights of an incoming car. He retrieves his portable radar gun from the back seat, getting himself ready to give the driver a little surprise. Holding the awkward detector up, he takes another drag of the smoke and grins.

A classic sedan zooms by, a late-60s Ford Thunderbird. Lance's position in the speed trap means the driver can't see him, and the beautiful car speeds away into the darkness.

Lance looks down at the speed indicator, nodding in approval at the "83 MPH" of the gorgeous automobile. He shakes his head, raising his voice in the rural night as he speaks to himself. "With a car that cool, you are free to go."

One cool thing about being a cop is you get to pronounce judgment so often. Even though there are rules for everything, much of the time what you do is at your own discretion and not subject to review, even by asshole sergeants. In this case, the car can go free. Lance imagines himself as some ancient Roman Emperor, giving his blessing to the speeding driver with a noble wave of his hand. Grinning at the imagined image, he laughs as he leans over the car's hood.

Another set of headlights arises in the darkness, and Lance's laughing dies down as it gets closer. He tenses in anticipation, noticing the car is really moving.

A modern Mercedes GLS SUV flies by, and it's one of those ultra-expensive types he's seen in some Bond film or other. A glance at the readout gives him a pleasant thrill: "92."

"Gotcha, ya rich fuck," says Lance, and his mood brightens even more. Nothing better than dispensing a little justice to some prick that'll drop a hundred and fifty grand on a car—even a nice one. After throwing his smoke to the side, Lance hops into the dark interior of his patrol car and spins off in pursuit.

Accelerating quickly, Lance doesn't take long to catch up to his new victim. The driver seems to have noticed the police attention and must be trying to act the part of a law-abiding driver by following the speed limit. *Not gonna happen, dude; I got ya dead-to-rights.*

Lance flicks on his strobed lights, lighting up the SUV with the many-colored emergency beams. The Mercedes driver slows down immediately, even turning on his blinker as he searches for a place to safely pull off the road.

Coming to a stop, Lance chuckles as he watches the car ahead. Reaching to the side, he pulls his ticket book from the door compartment. Clambering out of the car, he straightens himself and his gun belt before making his way toward the driver's window.

From behind the Mercedes, the view from the police camera catches everything. Placed at the precise location to enable all traffic stops to be recorded, the entirety of

CHAPTER ELEVEN

each public interaction is monitored to protect the police department from frivolous claims of abuse.

Lance advances to the SUV, his ticket book at the ready as he approaches. When he gets closer, the hum of driver's descending window reaches the police recording.

A voice comes from the unseen driver, sounding panicked. There's a slight Slavic accent to his speech. "I'm sorry, Officer. My wife is really sick; I need to get her to hospital."

Lance is immediately concerned. He reorients himself to the back driver-side window, tucking his ticket book away and taking out a flashlight. Trying to see inside, he taps on the glass and raises his voice. "Roll down the window."

As the window descends, Lance does a double-take, and confusion fills his face. "Shit, are you OK?"

Lance tries to open the door, but it's locked. He reaches deep inside, holding the flashlight up to get a better view.

Abruptly, there's a cracking sound, and Lance is pulled forcibly into the door. His gun hand is now inside, and he steadies himself with his other arm, trying to fight being pulled in.

Lance strains to get his arm back, but a horrible cracking, the sound of rending flesh, splits the night.

"Ahhhhh. Let go of my arm. Fuuuuckk!" screams Lance, and he redoubles his efforts to extricate himself as he braces against the door.

DESPICABLE

A horrible growling emerges from the inside of the car, like that of some horrid beast. There's also gnawing and splashing of blood that accompanies the guttural nightmare.

Lance is hysterical and terrified as he tugs back, trying to reclaim his arm. "Help me. Somebody help me...God, please."

Lance's powerful frame is pulled ever closer into the window frame, and the horrific wet sounds continue, even as he wails like a stricken child. He's soon close to being yanked entirely inside.

Except, there's no room for him to enter that way. His head and neck are too high, and his protests lessen as his body is bent backward. With a hideous cracking sound, his neck and spine are broken, and he's folded and pulled from view into the rear of the Mercedes.

The animal growls continue, but the grunts of the attack die away. Lance's feet now stick out of the window, with awkward muscle spasms forcing them to extend at an odd angle.

From the front seat, the driver climbs out. He is a brawny man dressed in a suit, but he otherwise appears normal. Stepping to Lance's feet, he notices an ankle holster on one of the protruding legs and stops to inspect it. He withdraws a small revolver from the backup leather holster, holding it up to the light admiringly. He slips the weapon into his pocket before casually pushing Lance's feet all the way into the vehicle. Once they are inside, the window rolls up, and no further sounds of Lance's torment or his vicious attackers are heard.

The driver walks back to the police car, where his form disappears from the camera view as he climbs into the driver's seat. When the police door slams shut, there's a pause as another man in the SUV gets out of the passenger door and crosses to the driver's side. This man is also dressed in a suit, and he calmly climbs into the SUV's driver side.

With that, the Mercedes pulls onto the road. The police lights are switched off, and the view from the camera cuts out just as the cop car follows the expensive vehicle down the dark road.

Chapter Twelve

The living room in Martin's house is well-lit and comfortable. Seth sits on a beige couch, eagerly looking up at a large-screen television mounted on the wall. On the coffee table in front of him lies his gaming console, and various wires and secondary controllers are jumbled in a heap next to it.

Walking into the room, Kalisa sets a tray full of cookies next to Seth, which distracts him just long enough to pop one of the nut and frosting-clad morsels into his mouth. Resuming his battle on the screen, he barely notices his mom's frown at his gaming fixation. He also ignores her hand as she picks at his curly hair affectionately. Sighing, Kalisa finds the remote and lowers the volume of his military battle before exiting the room.

When Kalisa walks into the kitchen, she sees her father at the table, a steaming cup of coffee cradled in his hands. He has a haggard look on his face, one that makes him look older than even his advanced years would indicate.

Kalisa can see that this man is worried, terrified over what's happening, but seemingly powerless to do anything about it. Martin has lived a life that's involved generous helpings of misery and mourning, and now his remaining child finds herself in some bizarre circumstance of missing people and unknown enemies. She gives him a caring smile as she sits, settling next to another coffee cup opposite him.

On the wall, a small TV plays the news in hushed tones, but neither of them pays much attention to it. Darkness from the windows shows that daytime is a recent memory.

Kalisa leans forward, affecting a warmth towards her dad that's been absent for several years. "Well, that was crazy. Baudin is one weird guy."

Martin nods a pained agreement, staring outside as he considers their encounter. "I think you mean 'scary'. Even for an old man, that wasn't an experience I had anticipated."

"What do you make of it, dad? He didn't seem like he wanted to hurt us…but there was something about him. We were the ones armed, and I got the feeling he wasn't too worried. That's not very reassuring."

"No, he didn't wish to hurt us, that much was clear," responds Martin, and he stares into his coffee, working through his thoughts. "But he wanted to warn us away,

CHAPTER TWELVE

like he knew something we don't. This is concerning, daughter, that events that affect you…and now my grandson, are unexplained."

Leaning back, Kalisa runs her finger around the rim of her cup, thinking through her father's words. "Well, let's start with what we do know. We have two people around me that have disappeared…and a funeral home full of rotten meat, whose owner, the creepiest dude I've ever met, is having me followed."

Remembering something, Kalisa stands and retrieves Martin's handkerchief from the counter, the one used to collect the green substance from the preparation room's cabinet at the mortuary. She places it on the table as she returns to her seat. They both raise a lip at the unpleasant substance.

"We also have…this," says Kalisa.

Martin gestures to the substance, playing the part of a skeptic. "That really could be anything. We don't know what chemicals are involved in that type of work. I'm not sure we would want to know what things are involved in preparing bodies for burial."

Kalisa doesn't look convinced. "That's true, but tell me you've ever heard of glowing green goop being used in anything. It looked like that crap from *Ghostbusters*."

Martin takes a moment to ponder, nodding a reluctant agreement. Some time passes as they consider what happened. Kalisa's frustration is palpable, and she broods over what any of it means.

Cocking his head, Martin suddenly remembers something, and he adopts a storyteller's voice as he focuses on Kalisa. "I never mentioned this, but my father once spoke to me about 'crazy things,' that he saw from his youth. I think he referred to them as 'unexplainable.'"

Standing up, Martin ambles over to peek into the living room, making sure Seth can't hear the conversation. The boy is embroiled with a raucous battle and duly preoccupied.

Martin returns to the kitchen, where he remains standing as he sorts through his memories. "During the 1960s, when your grandfather was fighting one war or another, he came to the belief that his men were being hunted in the jungle."

"Hunted? Like by an animal? A leopard…or lion?"

"No, he said it was by something else, something that was evil. Unnatural."

Kalisa looks doubtful and raises her eyebrows in surprise. "That doesn't sound like him like him at all."

"Agreed, daughter. I have never known a more pragmatic and well-grounded man in my life, but he was convinced there was something else out there. He said men would disappear on the edge of their encampments, always when they were alone."

"But in combat, men come up missing," says Kalisa, continuing her skeptical line of reasoning. "Or they get captured, maybe even desert their posts, right?

CHAPTER TWELVE

Martin grimaces and nods. "This is true, but I am not trying to convince you of devils or witches. I merely state that your grandfather was convinced there was something otherworldly involved. When the war was over, he never had that feeling again. But he always remembered that time as something he could not understand."

Abruptly, Kalisa's gaze shifts to the wall-mounted TV, where the news is playing. On the screen is a picture of Lance, where he's smiling from some banquet while in uniform. Grabbing the nearby remote, Kalisa raises the volume and stares with a disbelieving frown.

"...*all indications are he has simply vanished without a trace, along with his patrol car. Police say there will be no stone unturned until he is found, and a statewide search for the officer will continue night and day...*"

With a trembling hand, Kalisa mutes the remote. Looking up to Martin, she is shell-shocked.

Confused, Martin looks back and forth between the TV and his daughter. Realization moves across his aged features, and he gestures to the news program.

"Your boyfriend?" asks Martin.

Unable to answer, Kalisa merely nods, her eyes empty and lost.

#

DESPICABLE

The detective office is a picture of controlled chaos. Piles of folders, reports, and photos from various cases are stacked in maddening order around its confines, making the area appear like a hoarder's paradise. Even the chairs and simple couch in the corner of the space are used in the filing system, with stacks of documents covering all the available free space.

Detective Wiggins stands in the middle of the room, his eyes moving over his precise investigative filing system. Looking down, he studies a report in his hands, taking in each word of the writing with an engrossed focus.

Walking to his desk chair, he perches himself on its wooden frame, leaning back and continuing his study of the "For Official Use Only" paper.

There's a sudden knock at the door. Leaning forward, Wiggins isn't able to respond quick enough as it's flung open. Kalisa strides into the office, eyes wide and intense. She glares down at him, even as a flustered Sergeant Herrick follows in her wake.

"Kalisa, what are you doing here?" asks Wiggins, and he motions for Herrick to stop from dragging Kalisa bodily from the room. Herrick, a burly and intense man, huffs in disappointment.

Kalisa moves close, unafraid and placing her hands on his desk as she leans down. "I need to talk, Wiggins. I've got a ton to tell you, and you gotta listen to me. It's a matter of life and death."

CHAPTER TWELVE

Taken aback, Wiggins peers up to Kalisa, then over to Herrick. Perplexed, Wiggins raises his eyebrows in an unspoken question. After a moment of indecision, the detective motions to the door, and Herrick retreats back outside.

#

Wiggins stands with his arms crossed next to a bulletin board, where someone has scrawled *Eat your Wheaties* across the white background of the panel. His expression is puzzled, like he's waiting for a punchline that hasn't yet arrived.

"You…were having an affair with Officer Savini?"

Kalisa nods, foregoing the shame of her actions to get to the point. "Until about a month ago. I ended it when my husband found out."

"And you blackmailed him to run the plates of a…some mortician?"

Kalisa breathes deep, trying to be patient. She likes Wiggins, but if he doesn't get on with this, she's gonna slap him. "Funeral home owner, Mathias Baudin. He's been having cars follow me all over Reno."

Sighing, Wiggins grabs a notepad and sits at his desk. He begins writing, using his pen to etch each word carefully, like it's an official medieval document. "And you also knew this boy you say was missing? The one who has petty arrests? Eddie…"

"Orlovsky," Kalisa says, rolling her eyes with irritation at the slow pace of his penmanship. "He's a good kid. I'm worried about him."

It takes Wiggins a while longer to finish his notes. Kalisa's eye bulge with impatience as he finally closes the pad and looks up. He's clearly enjoying the deliberative approach to questioning her, and he kicks his feet on the desk as he stares up.

"You're not stupid, Kalisa, I think we can both agree on that. You know you're the only person tied to two separate...victims?"

Kalisa agrees with a humorless smile, not particularly caring about his insinuation. "Yeah, but I'm not here to confess anything; I'm here to help. This funeral home dude is tied to these disappearances—he has to be."

Kalisa steps close to the desk, and Wiggins cocks a surprised eye in response. She withdraws her father's green-glop handkerchief from a pocket, setting it in front of Wiggins. "And we found this at the funeral home when we visited yesterday. You need to get it analyzed; I've never seen anything like it."

Lowering his feet, Wiggins leans close to the dried green substance. Looking disgusted, he reaches into his desk and withdraws an evidence bag. Using his pen, he drops it into the bag, then sets it aside.

Sighing, he stands, stepping close to Kalisa and offering her a shark's smile. "Everything you say will be

CHAPTER TWELVE

checked, that you can be certain of. But…I do have one question for you."

"What is it?"

"Would you be willing to take a polygraph?" asks Wiggins, and a smirk crosses his features, expecting her to avoid incriminating herself further.

Kalisa doesn't flinch from the suspicion. *This bastard thinks I'm gonna lawyer up.*

Kalisa nods, her face self-confident and unafraid. "Anything it takes to figure this out. Anything."

#

Alex is a hulking man, and he leans over the metal cart as he pushes it down a long hallway. His bald skull is shiny and well-kept, almost to the point of being waxed, and he peers ahead with a bored expression. Below him is the outline of a bulky corpse, hidden under a sheet laid across the noisy gurney.

Alex's annoying cart squeaks as he aims it down the hall. Distant double doors of a room wait for him, light peaking through its windows. His pace is neither hurried nor lazy as he makes his way ahead, focusing with disinterested eyes.

He pushes his way through the set of doors, emerging into a wide and open sterile area. The space here has several tables and looks like an operating room in a hospital. At the end of the room against the far wall is an

DESPICABLE

enormous scale. Wayne stands next to the scale, and he is of similar height and age to Alex, looking almost like a twin overgrown baby. His impatient demeanor fills his face with a grouchy and obnoxious expression.

"Come on," says Wayne, and his sour expression grows an even bigger scowl. "We've got a client waiting his turn."

Alex nods absently. He moves the sheet aside on the cart, revealing an ugly frozen pig. The dead animal is dark, with matted whiskers and a glistening, bloody snout.

Alex hefts the animal with a grunt and carries it to the large scale, plunking it on the large steel plate of the weighing tray. He murmurs to his impatient coworker with a deadpan shrug. "Yeah, well…they can afford to be patient."

Wayne stares down at the fetid pig, pursing his lips as he peers at the beast's registered weight. Meeting Alex's gaze, he shakes his head and reaches down behind the scale, lifting a huge machete.

Wayne cleaves into the half-frozen animal, chopping bits of the creature off. The ferocity of the strikes is jarring.

Alex doesn't seem to notice or care.

Finally, Wayne hacks most of the head off, and he follows up by pushing the detached flesh to the floor.

Wayne holds up the machete, pumping the air in silent triumph as he points to the scale. "I always get the weight right. I'm a genius at this."

CHAPTER TWELVE

Rolling his eyes, Alex mock-claps his large hands together, feigning a "you're my hero" expression. "It's good you have such lofty goals in life."

Alex ignores Wayne's pissed-off face, and he grins to himself about the non-subtle insult to his colleague. Reaching up, Alex grabs the side of rotting pork and hauls it back to the creaking gurney. Covering the dead animal again with the sheet, he exits the room, leaving behind a fuming Wayne to clean up the mess.

Retracing his way down the hall, Alex turns right in a different direction than he came. Looking ahead, there is a huge metal door, one that looks as sturdy as the gates of Fort Knox. Alex stops in front of it, looking the old metal up and down.

Reaching into his pocket, Alex withdraws an old-looking key and fits it into the door's lock. With a great click, he disengages the mechanism and swings the groaning doors open.

Inside, the lights go on automatically, and a large crematorium is revealed. The room has several large ovens, with a conveyor belt leading to each of the brick-lined incineration areas.

At the center oven, there's a cheap open coffin perched on the conveyor. Its lid is open, awaiting a new resident. Pushing the cart inside, Alex stops next to the belt and hefts the pig inside the open casket. It takes some time to arrange the misshapen animal inside, but Alex is finally able to close the fleshy hog inside.

DESPICABLE

Happy, Alex strides to a bank of controls on the wall, where there's a set of old-fashioned switches and thick buttons.

Taking a moment to rest, Alex withdraws a back of thick bubble gum from his pocket. He unwraps several portions of the chunky substance, popping one after another into his mouth.

As he works his jaw over the huge glob of gum, he slaps a button on the wall. The conveyor belt starts up, and the coffin and its unfortunate animal make its way into the waiting fire.

Chapter Thirteen

Dr. Bergstrom sits in his chair, pen in hand and held at eye level as he stares ahead. His face is a mishmash of shock and runaway worry. Blinking several times, he tries to focus his train of thought.

"So...wh...what you're saying is—."

"That I'm completely fucked," responds Kalisa, and after the interruption, she gives him a little smile, as if to say *it's par for the course in my life*. Sitting in her normal place on the couch, she regards Bergstrom with a friendly demeanor reserved for only a few people in her chaotic life.

Truth is, there are some beneficial aspects to the problems in her insane life. First, that these disappearances are happening outside her own mind tells her she isn't crazy, which is always reassuring. The second thing is she has had a lifetime of shit sandwiches to eat, so it's not like she's overwhelmed by another ring of the excrement dinner bell.

Bergstrom manages to claw his way back to rationality, and he raises his voice, trying to inject some normalcy into the session. "This is quite a situation you find yourself in. But none of these missing acquaintances are actually known to be harmed, correct?"

Kalisa tilts her head, fixing Bergstrom with a skeptical stare. "Doc, if you believe three people disappearing means they're in great health, then your degrees aren't worth much."

Bergstrom sets his pen inside his notebook and closes it on his lap. His mood has decidedly taken a turn for the worse, and for the first time, something like whining replaces his know-it-all disposition. "Then, perhaps you should get the police involved? They are equipped to deal with such—."

"Already done. I've reported everything. I just hope they aren't as useless as normal."

Bergstrom is relieved, perhaps thinking he doesn't have to report it himself. He rallies his mental forces for an attempt at salvaging Kalisa's emotional health. "I am worried what this will all do to your well-being, Kalisa. Do you have any support within your family, or friends? Such help will be of immense importance for your continued improvement."

Kalisa reaches into her pocket and takes out a package of Tic Tacs. Thumbing a few into her mouth, she looks unworried and carefree as she sucks on them. Bergstrom notices the unconcerned gesture with a frown.

CHAPTER THIRTEEN

"My dad is helping me," says Kalisa. "Me and Seth have moved in with him until this crazy shit is over. We're trying to stay under the radar."

Kalisa stands and looks down at the concerned mental health professional. "Doc, I'm really here for another reason: you."

Bergstrom grows defensive. Rising from his chair, he notably keeps some distance from Kalisa as he straightens himself. "What do you mean?"

"Well, I'm going to be taking a break from our chats for a while," explains Kalisa. "You must know I have more important things to deal with."

"I don't think that's a good idea, Kalisa. You need to stay grounded in your life, and our time together—."

"So, I wanted you to be careful."

Silence fills the room, and Bergstrom doesn't have a clue what Kalisa is talking about. It's like he has become the novice in their verbal sessions.

Kalisa holds up three fingers, and she motions out the window with her other hand. "Three people that I've been in touch with or known are missing. Three. Now, you are another person I've been around, so I wanted to warn you. It's just common sense."

"I assure you, there's no danger..."

Kalisa juts her hand out, causing Bergstrom to flinch. He may be brilliant, but a physically imposing man he is not.

"I just felt I had to warn you, Doc," Kalisa says, and she clasps his limp hand in a hearty shake. "I couldn't live with myself if something happened to you."

Kalisa claps Bergstrom on the shoulder, motioning her head to the door. "I gotta go, but watch your back. Please."

As Kalisa disengages and walks out the door, Bergstrom nods bravely, downplaying her warning. Before leaving completely, she gives him an affectionate smile and nods another goodbye.

When she's gone from the office area, Bergstrom stares nervously after her. Re-seating himself, he's suddenly less cozy in his relaxing work environment.

#

Rolling hills of desert foliage jut out from the flat plains of the high desert, moving in a rough line towards a higher set of mountains to the south of Reno. A two-lane highway ascends these scattered ridges, following a historical route traveled by prospectors and wealth-seekers, people that carved a living from the unrefined wild areas that make up the bulk of Nevada's remote landscape.

Kalisa climbs this isolated road in her car, peering out the windows as she passes shrubs and scenery that haven't changed since long before settlers discovered its hidden mineral wealth. Kalisa has heard that the famous

CHAPTER THIRTEEN

"Comstock Lode," a rich vein of silver mined from the area, played a key role in financing the Civil War, but looking at the never-ending sparse hills now doesn't make her think of wealth.

Instead, the area and its history can be a little depressing. Poor miners that toiled and died chasing their dreams of extreme fortunes is one disheartening thing, but so is the idea of the Natives whose own stories weren't written down. In fact, the region was inhabited by scattered bands of Indians for thousands of years, and Kalisa laments that those long-dead histories have no easy way of being accessed. It's crazy to her way of thinking that the power of supercomputers has been condensed into mobile phones, but current culture is still so unaware of so many lives that preceded it.

But it's also true Mark Twain made his career in the early 1860s in nearby Virginia City, so at least this area has that going for it. His real name was Samuel Clemens, and he worked as a local newspaper reporter, but Kalisa always loved the famous author's novels, as well as his cool whiskers. Sometimes you just gotta look for some good points in history, otherwise, your outlook will always be bleak and dreary.

Coming around a bend in the empty highway, Kalisa focuses on a dirt road to the side as she slows down her venerable car. Little more than a track, she reads a sign to the side that proclaims *Trespassers will be shot, and survivors will be prosecuted*. Grinning, she aims her car down the

DESPICABLE

dusty trail and relaxes at having found the entrance to the property.

She gently drives this dirt track for a few minutes, bouncing over roots and rocks as she moves deeper into the private property. Each turn of the dusty pathway brings a brighter smile to her lips, and her anticipation builds with each turn in the unpaved road.

A final turn brings a mobile home into view, one that is tidy and somehow appropriate to the wild mountain scenery in the background. But, it's also apparent from the home's remoteness that visitors are probably a rare occurrence.

The front door from the mobile opens, and Darryl, her longtime colleague from work, exits with a big grin. He still hasn't managed to remove his whiskers, but that smile and unshaven face has brightened her otherwise sad days on more than one occasion. Friends are rare in her life, and she cherishes each one, whatever their shortcomings.

As Kalisa gets out of her car, Darryl descends the steps of his wooden front porch, his smile growing wider. They shake with obvious friendliness, the kind reserved for people that know and accept each other.

"Darryl, thanks for letting me visit…and listening to my problems," Kalisa says, and she notes he at least combed his hair for the visit.

"No problemo, my friend. I can always make time for you, you know that."

CHAPTER THIRTEEN

There's an awkward silence as Kalisa takes in the surroundings, her gaze falling over various unidentifiable rusting machinery in the front yard and a distant homemade shooting range with paper targets draped over bales of hay.

Keeping his smile, Darryl motions to the trailer, and they pace towards his home.

Inside, the place is spiffy, as it looks to have seen a recent attempt at vacuuming and dusting the wooden furniture. A vase of real flowers even sits on a glass coffee table in the living area, where two large screen TVs are bolted and pointed towards a dark couch.

An assortment of conspiracy-themed photos adorn the walls, and one frame in the connected kitchen-front room states *It's not paranoia if it's true.* Darryl's self-conscious smile shows he wants to be proud of his home, and Kalisa obliges him by nodding her approval.

Stepping in the kitchen, Kalisa is surprised to see an AR-15 lying on the table. Darryl offers a grin in response, not bashful about the weapon's presence or several boxes of 5.56-millimeter ammunition stacked next to it.

"Nice place, Darryl," says Kalisa. "Looks like you're ready for the zombie apocalypse."

Darryl shakes his head, pointing across the room to a crude photo of a photoshopped-looking flying saucer. "Zombies aren't real. Those are."

Kalisa shrugs, not inclined to argue about the existence of anything crazy at this point.

DESPICABLE

Darryl catches himself, remembering the purpose of her visit. "You're gonna love this."

Darryl moves by Kalisa and walks to the back of the trailer. Out of sight, he bangs around for a while as he looks for something.

Emerging with a brown shopping bag, Darryl sets it next to the carbine on his kitchen table. Looking expectantly at Kalisa, he motions for her to look inside.

Reaching in, Kalisa pulls out a huge revolver. It's wrapped in a funny holster, one that's intended to be strapped on the small of a person's back. It barely fits in her hand, despite having a short barrel.

Darryl gestures to the gun, speaking like he's bragging about his child acing a standardized test. "That's a .454 Casull—more powerful than most hunting rifles. And only a 2.75-inch barrel."

Kalisa pulls the gun out of its holster. She checks the empty cylinder to see that it's unloaded, then hefts the weighty weapon as she aims down the sight into the living room.

Snapping his fingers at having forgotten something, Darryl reaches into a cabinet near the microwave. He rummages around, pulling out another box of ammunition and setting it on the table. "I used to carry that gun when I lived in Alaska. It'll stop a grizzly with one shot. Did you know there's thirty thousand grizzlies in Alaska?"

CHAPTER THIRTEEN

Kalisa cocks her head at that factoid, reminding herself never to vacation there. The thought of blizzards is off-putting enough, but sharing space with man-eating bears, no matter how much the danger is exaggerated, crosses it entirely off her list. Sighing, she pushes the revolver back in the holster and returns it to the bag.

Darryl continues on. "It kicks like a mule, and the rounds are like two bucks each, so go easy on 'em unless you really need to let loose."

Kalisa focuses on Darryl with an appreciative grin. She reaches down to dig into her purse, but Daryl shakes his head, not having any of it. "No way. I never charge friends, and you've always been a good one to me me. You're one of the few people that don't laugh at my…ideas."

Kalisa's appreciation grows wider, and for a moment she doesn't know what to say. "Darryl, I've always found that good people come in all varieties—and all beliefs. You're a stand-up guy, and I'm lucky to have you as a friend."

The camaraderie of the moment is powerful, but Darryl's smile wilts as his thoughts drift elsewhere. "I didn't want to tell you. I know you're going through a lot, but…Ben from work is missing."

"What?"

"Yeah, while you took a few days off, he stopped coming to work. Someone went to his place, and nobody can find him."

Disbelieving, Kalisa covers her face with her hands. She rubs her eyes, looking up at the ceiling. "Who would hurt Ben? He's the nicest guy I've ever met."

"Agreed," says Darryl, and he takes a step forward, lowering his voice so his words will sound authoritative. All traces of happiness have left his expression. "Kalisa, this is a crazy world, and only the prepared survive. I think you should get ready, 'cuz something is happening around you. I can feel it."

Kalisa can't believe someone new is missing from her life. Stepping to the front room, she nervously rubs her hands through her hair as she considers what a wonderful man her friend Ben was. She processes what any of it could mean, trying to focus on what matters in her tortured life. "I'll…do that. I'm gonna take some more time off to protect my family. I've got to figure out what the fuck is going on. Would you do me a favor?"

Darryl nods vigorously, his face determined and honest. "Anything. You name it."

Kalisa gestures to his rifle and ammunition on the table. "Take that everywhere with you. And please…be safe."

#

Seth sits at Martin's kitchen table, eyes focused down. Below him is a large sheet of thick paper, and he's drawing on it with his tongue out in concentration. With

CHAPTER THIRTEEN

a mess of colored pencils at his side, he's halfway through a rendition of some large monster from one of his horror movies. For a young artist, it's pretty good, with white fangs, hairy unkempt body hair, and yellow, cat-like eyes.

"I'm gonna have to ban you from scary movies," says Kalisa, and she affectionately pats him on the shoulder as she peers from behind his back. "That doesn't look like something I'd like to run into."

Undeterred, Seth stays quiet while he continues with his masterpiece.

Leaving him to his drawing, Kalisa moves to the living room. Her father sits on the couch, reading a weathered old hardcover book. She notices the title, *Myths of Central Africa*, with a frown. Martin sets the book aside when he notices her standing there.

Kalisa gets straight to the point. "Dad, we can't stay in this house. We're sitting ducks."

Martin gives her an uncertain gaze, gesturing to the house around them. "Tell me, daughter, where we won't be 'sitting ducks.'"

Kalisa thinks for a moment, mentally rummaging through her options before deciding. "Grandpa's cabin, up by Tahoe. Nobody knows where it's at, and we can defend it without hurting innocent people. It's perfect for our needs, assuming you agree."

Looking intrigued, Martin thinks it over, then nods. "But how will we defend it, exactly?"

Kalisa points to the corner of the room, where a shotgun leans against the wall. "In any way possible, with whatever we need to do. We'll kill whatever is after us, 'cuz I'm never gonna be a victim again."

Martin fixes Kalisa with an admiring smile. He is surprised by her bravado, but he's also clearly happy with her attitude. He stares at her with genuine respect, and for once in a very long time he looks at his daughter with pride.

#

The diner is not busy, with only a few people picking at their greasy food throughout the place. Elevator music accompanies the 50s motif of the restaurant, and a gaudy red jukebox sits unused in the corner of the brightly lit establishment. Darkness peaks through the windows, showcasing a barely lit parking lot.

Rick sits in a corner booth, a cup of coffee and open menu next to him. He stares down at his mobile phone, surfing listlessly through the Internet with a scowl on his face.

Kalisa walks close to the table, stepping carefully, like she wants to avoid an encounter with a pit bull. Rick sees her in his peripheral vision but makes a show of ignoring her approach. Each in their own way is sizing the other up, but for what purpose neither seems to know.

"Rick? Can I sit down?" Kalisa asks.

CHAPTER THIRTEEN

"You're the one who wanted to meet. Have at it," Rick responds, and he motions across the table. Notably, Kalisa notices he's on the other side of the booth, leaving no room for her to scoot next to him. She can't blame him, but she's still disappointed.

Kalisa slides in across from Rick. Her eyes are clear as she talks, and she fixates directly on her husband. "I've asked to meet in public, because things aren't too good right now in my life. Could hardly be worse, in fact."

"I saw that. I noticed on the news your boyfriend is missing. Did that cocksucker run off with some other married woman?"

Kalisa is taken aback by the intensity of his bitterness, but she can't say she's surprised. With men, infidelity often strikes like an earthquake at their soul. Whereas women typically focus on the emotions involved, the physical act of cheating is something not easily forgotten by males. She could never be described as a wise person, but she recognizes the need to tread carefully.

"He doesn't concern me," says Kalisa, acting indifferent. "What bothers me is other people are coming up missing around me, and I have no idea why."

This admission gets Rick's attention, and he straightens up. "Is Seth OK? Where—."

"He's fine. He's with me or my dad around the clock. I took him out of school; told them we have a family emergency, which isn't lying."

Rick stews for a moment, trying to make sense of what's happening. "What's going on, Swee…Kalisa? Who the hell did you piss off?"

Rick almost calling her "sweetie" brightens Kalisa's spirits. In spite of the precarious situation, she feels hopeful as she continues. "I don't really know, and I never did anything to anyone that I can think of. Somebody's been following me, so dad and I are gonna leave town for a few days until shit calms down."

"If you're thinking you're gonna take Seth—."

"Relax, I'd never put him in danger," says Kalisa, gently interrupting. "I'm gonna leave him with you, if that's OK. With one request."

Rick raises an eyebrow in response but is otherwise quiet.

"Please go to your mom's and borrow or buy a gun. I…don't know if you'll also be followed, so you shouldn't go home from here. My father will meet you at your mom's tomorrow morning with Seth."

Rick considers the plan. He's confused but agrees with a tilt of his head. "How long will you be up there?"

"Don't know, but if whoever this is follows us, he's gonna be one dead fucker."

Rick smiles grimly at her intentions, impressed with her drive to protect her family.

Kalisa continues, lowering her voice to soften her words. "And Rick, please consider forgiving me. I'm miserable without you…I don't want anyone else."

CHAPTER THIRTEEN

There's a pause as Rick takes in the unexpected request. He meets her eyes with vicious intensity, but there's also no hatred there. "Forgiving is one thing…but trusting you ever again. I don't know."

Kalisa is ecstatic to not be rejected outright. She changes the subject, moving to capitalize on the moment. "Remember your dream of buying a new truck and a fifth wheel? So we could travel around the country and visit different campgrounds?"

"You mean the dream we could never do because you pissed all our money away in the casinos?" Rick asks, but he smiles a little, no mean intent in his words.

Kalisa takes the hit in stride, acknowledging the truth with a sad grin before going on. "Maybe we could find a way to do that when this is over? Go anywhere you want, for however long you want."

Rick leans back and puts his arms on the top of the booth, assuming a contemplative position. Silence continues for several moments before he speaks slowly, parsing his words. "I don't know, Kalisa. We'll have to wait and see."

After a pause, Rick lowers his arms and sips the last of his coffee. He rises from the booth and motions his head toward the door. Without saying more, he grabs his keys from the table and nods a goodbye.

On his way out, Kalisa watches him go, considering where they went wrong, and how they can recapture their shared past. They really were a great couple, but could they ever be again?

Chapter Fourteen

Martin stares at a photo on his bedroom wall. His eyes are glazed over and removed to a distant time, rummaging through old memories and experiences that tickle at the back of his brain. He doesn't weep or cry, because all the tears and heartbreak from that long-removed period have been tapped out; the human mind can only endure so much stress and heartbreak before it folds into itself, either choosing to survive by numbing itself to psychological agony—or receding into catatonic slumber.

The photo is of he and his wife Marie standing in front of a forceful waterfall in the midday sun. Green trees and mist from the roiling river fill the area around, forcing them to squint into the photo. She is beautiful and carefree, smiling and clinging to his arm as they as if she could be swept away in the torrid rapids behind them. Trouble is, they would be swept away by something else a few years later, a genocide that would claim the lives of more than a half-million people in his beloved homeland, Rwanda.

Their trip to Rusumo Falls had been at a high point in his life, a time when the world had seemed so right, full of possibilities and hope. Such a simple thing as a basic photo from a long-lost cheap camera allows him to access those feelings, making his eyes misty as he stands here, half-a-world away and almost three decades removed.

Shrugging away his burgeoning sorrow, Martin steps back and looks at his simple bed, looking down at some luggage thrown over the bedding. Reaching down, he grabs a large sheath from the interior of a garment bag. An enormous knife is revealed with a *Schünk* as he pulls it out, and its wicked blade glints in the dim light of the bedroom. With enough force, the razor-sharp fighting knife looks like it could gut a rhinoceros—or anything else he saw fit to butcher.

Martin had always had a fondness for knives, and he had always made sure to carry one when he was in areas where predatory animals could be on the hunt. With a grimace, he realizes that time for defensive caution has re-emerged, right here in the most normal of American cities.

Martin sets his jaw defiantly and runs the sheath of the knife onto his belt, taking his time to position it on his strong side for easy access. Pulling his coat on, he makes sure it's not easily noticeable as he appraises himself in his bedroom mirror. With a grunt, he lifts the packed bags

CHAPTER FOURTEEN

and leaves his room, teetering from the weight as he moves down the hallway.

When he emerges into the front room, Martin sees Kalisa preparing some sandwiches in the kitchen. Ever the doting mother, she neatly places the food in front of Seth, along with a tall glass of milk. Seth is engrossed in a hand-held video game, and he grabs the bread and nibbles from the crust without regard to its contents.

Seeing Martin standing there, Kalisa moves to hold the front door open for her father, and she offers him an appreciative smile on his way out to the car. He doesn't return the smile, but he does feel good at being useful, even if it just means packing their things for the trip.

When Martin has departed, Kalisa returns to her son, where she continues her overwatch of his meal. "Seth, we'll just be gone a few days. We just have a few things to take care of."

Leaning down, Kalisa gives him a smothering kiss, throwing him off from his game. She speaks into his ear as he frowns from the distraction. "Besides, your dad always lets you get away with more than I do, so you'll have a good time without boring mom around."

Oblivious to anything that could be wrong in the world, Seth merely peers up and smiles.

Kalisa walks to the counter, where she picks up a thick schoolbook, hefting it to look at its title, *Advanced Chemistry*. She turns it over in her hands, thinking for some time. Turning to Seth, she sets it next to his plate, smiling down at the deeply intelligent boy.

"Seth, before we go, maybe you can help me. Maybe you can give your mom some tips on how to make something?"

#

Wiggins stands in his office, surrounded by a sea of papers and folders. He stands watch over the collection of reports and interviews, looking for something particular in the midst the filing mess.

"Sergeant Herrick," Wiggins calls out, his annoyed voice rising to be heard through the open door. "Can you come in?"

After a few moments, Herrick peeks his own irritated face through the door. "Yeah?"

Frustrated, Wiggins stares down at his desk, digging through a stack of printed lab reports. "Can you call the lab and ask when we're getting those results? It's taking forever."

"Already did," replies Herrick. "They said they're waiting for the final tests."

Puzzled, Wiggins tilts his head to the side. "What the hell does that mean? What 'final tests?'"

Stepping fully into view, Herrick shrugs. "No idea. But you're welcome to call them yourselves, that way you

CHAPTER FOURTEEN

can yell at them when you still don't understand their answer."

It's quiet for a moment, and Herrick smirks while Wiggins frowns.

"What about the interview room?" asks Wiggins, changing the subject. "Do we have those interviews scheduled for our witnesses? I'm eager to see how full of shit Mrs. Nigimi is."

Herrick crosses his arms, looking doubtful. "She passed the polygraph. What else do you want?"

Wiggins scowls, shaking his head. "The biggest Russian spy of the Cold War passed them multiple times. It's mostly BS to get people to confess; there's a reason they can't be admitted in most court cases."

Herrick shrugs again, then exits from the office, letting the door slide shut behind him.

Walking from file to stacked folder, Wiggins begins stacking and re-stacking various papers. Over the next several minutes he brings the paperwork into proper order, finally stopping when everything is again to his liking.

Contented, Wiggins breathes deep, glad to have the universe of office organization in proper alignment.

A quick knock at the door, and it swings in abruptly. Theodore Brosius stands there, smiling and amicable. In his mid-fifties, he has impossibly white teeth and skin, and he looks like the Captain America of politicians. He steps into Wiggins' office unbidden.

Shocked, Wiggins stares at the stranger. "Who the fuck are you?"

Continuing his smile, Brosius extends his hand in greeting. When Wiggins ignores the friendly gesture, Brosius shrugs and turns around to close the door. After lowering the office blinds, he turns back to the bewildered detective.

Brosius speaks with a Swedish accent, but his pronunciation is perfect. "I'm Theodore Brosius, from the governor's office…and we really need to talk."

#

Later, Sergeant Herrick stands outside Wiggins' office. He leans down, trying to see inside the room through the corner of the drawn blinds. Frustrated, Herrick straightens himself and looks at his watch. He licks his lips and mumbles to himself.

"What in the hell…?"

The door springs open, and Brosius stands there, giving him a shrewd glare, like he knows all of Herrick's inner thoughts.

Brosius leans close to the sergeant, an affable look on his face. "Sergeant Herrick, I presume? I've always thought it rather impolite to eavesdrop. Wouldn't you agree?"

Herrick stares down at the much shorter man, his mouth open in rapt confusion. Unsure of himself,

CHAPTER FOURTEEN

Herrick stays quiet as he studies the pasty-faced visitor. When they lock gazes, it's Herrick that looks away first.

Reassuming a broad smile, Brosius sidesteps Herrick and strides past him in the hallway. As he paces away, his bounces with each step, overflowing with self-assured and bountiful energy. Not a concern in the world bothers the departing stranger, and that leaves Herrick with an uneasy feeling, like he just sidestepped a freight train.

Looking back to the office, Herrick steps inside it, his cautious and worried eyes seeking out Wiggins. He pulls the door shut behind, not knowing why, but suddenly feeling the need for a private conversation with his boss and old friend.

Wiggins sits at his desk, his face buried in his hands. He is silent as Herrick creeps closer, but he pulls his hands away when the sergeant gets within a few feet. Wiggins' face looks like a Holocaust survivor, with all the blood having left his normally expressive features.

"You don't want to know," says Wiggins, answering the unspoken question. "In one hundred years, you wouldn't want to know."

Wiggins covers his face with his hands again, rubbing his eyes before running them through his sandy-blond hair. Taking calculated breaths, he tries to control himself as he drones out his words. "Cancel all the interviews we scheduled."

Chapter Fifteen

Kalisa squints into the afternoon sun, peering out the dirty windshield of her car. Ahead of her is a long line of slower vehicles on a two-lane highway. Struggling to get enough speed, she eases into the passing lane and presses up the steep grade.

Around the ascending roadway is a beautiful site: snow-capped mountains and plush forests of pine trees. Intermittent rocky outcroppings break the monotonous woods that stretch toward the distant peaks of the Sierra Nevada Mountain Range, providing a stunning backdrop of eternal beauty.

In the passenger seat, Martin stares out, transfixed by the gorgeous scenery. "Your mother would have loved this area. It's majestic. A different beauty than Rwanda, but beauty just the same."

Kalisa nods her agreement as the car struggles past a fuel truck on the incline. "Yeah, and if not for those devils, she could be here with us. We would've had a lifetime…"

Kalisa's words drift off into her ceaseless grief, and she struggles to contain herself.

Martin keeps his eyes on the imposing mountains out his side window, his measured voice picking up where she left off. "You're right, of course. But you have to ask yourself something after all these years: would your mother want you to continue ruining your life over it? Evil found its way into our home so long ago, and until we see your mom and brother again, are we to let the monsters win? Even after three decades?"

Martin moves his gaze inside, and he looks directly over to Kalisa. "Daughter, you are too smart to let those despicable people have their way with you and Seth's life. And…my son-in-law's. You must make your way ahead—you have a bright future."

Kalisa doesn't quite know what to say. She starts to speak but is unable to counter her father's wisdom. She stays quiet as the passing lane ends and they make it to the top of a snow-laden ridge.

As the car reaches the crest of the mountain, they look out over an enormous lake below. Lake Tahoe, a crystal-clear body of mountain water, stretches into the distance, surrounded by looming mountain peaks. Almost two million years since its creation by shifting mountains, it's a timeless testament to the short timespans of humanity. Somehow, knowing this makes Kalisa feel a little better, that her life will blink on and off before the striking scenery even notices she was there.

CHAPTER FIFTEEN

Grimacing, Kalisa shakes away such thoughts, trying to fight the fatalism that constantly claws at her mind. Her pain and self-imposed misery cannot override the fact that she has the most beautiful son in the world, and she knows she has to live for him at least. And perhaps...for Rick, the one person who ever believed in her and made her feel special.

The vehicle continues its descent down a long ridgeline, with precipitous cliffs to the side providing breathtaking views of a pristine valley. Ahead, the dark splotch of a tunnel is hewn from the rocky slope, and shadows of the enclosed path envelop them in darkness as they drive through it.

When the car emerges into the light at the far end, Kalisa feels strange for a moment, like she's being watched. Looking over to her dad, she sees he is fixated on her, and he has something rarely witnessed in her life: an adoring smile, the smile of a loving father.

#

Some time later, they drive through a flat area at the bottom of a valley, one that is deep within extended clusters of trees and scattered pockets of frozen snow. The highway is not busy, and only the occasional car swooshes by.

Slowing down, Kalisa holds her phone up as she looks for a particular turnoff from the highway. The built-in mapping system is convenient, but she frowns at her ability to actually use it correctly. She never could quite figure out how GPS coordinates work, but now would be a good time for training. Glancing over, she notices her sleeping father, who grabs a nap with his head leaning against the frosty window.

Sighing, Kalisa doesn't want to wake him, so she slows down, half-driving on the pavement as looks for a break in the trees.

"Ha," Kalisa shouts, and she's rewarded by Martin lulling his head awake. "Found it."

Martin focuses ahead, blinking away sleep and nodding with satisfaction. Kalisa found the correct path to their cabin, and that's clearly more than he expected. Straightening himself from his slumber, he pushes his glasses up his nose and focuses ahead.

Proud of her navigation skills, Kalisa turns onto a dirt road, one that's barely traceable within the forest and its millions of pine needles and cones. She drives carefully around copses of trees and dead brush, making her way farther into the deepening woods.

#

Pop music drifts through the preparation room at Baudin's Funeral Home. The soft beats and head-pumping bass of a forgotten 80's hair band are pumped from speakers attached to the walls, as well as the

CHAPTER FIFTEEN

hallways outside. Unlike the constant mournful tunes that usually serenade visitors to the business, the lively if unrecognizably bland lyrics resound throughout the establishment.

Mathias Baudin stands over an unseen corpse at one of the metal tables, moving his head to the beat with carefree enjoyment. Below, his arms gyrate with the fluctuating rhythm, and a squishing sound accompanies the unintelligible lyrics of the upbeat tune.

Mathias slows his juking enjoyment as he bears down, pressing his weight upon the body. More squishing comes from the below him, and further stripping of flesh occurs, sounding something like masking tape being peeled from a dry surface.

Pulling back from his unknown patient, Mathias holds his arms up, much like a surgeon announcing the completion of an operation. His scrub suit is covered in blood and undefinable body fluids, while his hands are covered in a combination of those liquids with a green sheen of glowing muck.

Mathias turns to the back of the room, where Stefan waits, his face a mask of disinterested professionalism. Young and spry, Stefan has a bearing decades older than his youthful face would indicate.

"It never gets any easier, does it?" asks Mathias.

Stefan merely nods in response, his glum features unwilling or uninterested to respond.

A knock from the entry door gets Mathias' attention, and he turns to see Kevin waving for his attention from the edge of the dark hallway. As bulky as a powerlifter, Kevin looks a bit ridiculous in his tight suit, like it was stretched to fit around his bulky frame.

Kevin motions to his ear to indicate the need to be heard. Mathis picks up a nearby remote to mute the distracting sound, leaving the controller covered with the gel of mixed body fluids when he sets it back down.

"Yes?"

Kevin speaks in a squeaky voice, one that would Mike Tyson's gravelly in comparison. "They've vacated their home. Nobody can find them."

Mathias rolls his eyes, taking a moment to collect himself. It's hard enough to be in charge of things, but harder yet when Laurel and Hardy are in charge of surveillance. "I was afraid of that. I'm never surprised by what they do, but why is it so difficult to anticipate their reluctance to let us follow them?"

Kevin goes quiet, and his worried gaze drifts to the floor, like avoiding an answer will make the question go away.

"I don't need to tell you how important it is that they are found," continues Mathias. "Get whoever you need, whatever you need, but LOCATE them now. I won't have more attention brought to this, either by the authorities or our own…associates."

CHAPTER FIFTEEN

Kevin nods and pivots from the room, disappearing down the hallway as the doors swing shut.

When he's gone, Mathias' eyes flash an intense yellow, giving him a vicious appearance. Breathing deep, he controls himself and glances down at his work. "These things we do are necessary, but nevertheless sad."

Looking back up, Mathias' eyes are again normal, and he moves his gaze to Stefan. "This one is ready. Bring the next."

Stefan steps close. With a grunt, he flops the body to a gurney with a slopping sound. As he pushes it toward the double doors, the exposed leg of the corpse becomes visible. Down the leg and foot of the flesh are a series of long cuts, and copious quantities of green jelly encase the dead flesh in a translucent slime.

#

The small cabin is well built, consisting of sturdy logs set in a firm foundation. An attractive porch runs the front of it, and the rustic vibe is enhanced by thickets of trees that surround the isolated getaway. Several hundred yards from its front lies a small lake, which glistens in the morning light. Birds chirp from a thousand places in the remote surrounding forest.

Only a few yards from the cabin, Kalisa leans from the top of a ladder, extending a trimmer up one of the trees. Taking her time, she saws through a thick branch, watching it drop to the ground with a triumphant grin.

Her father sits on a tree stump not far away, and he nods at the fresh tree limb. He has a stack of sticks around him, all of which have been sharpened into crude spears and stakes. He clutches his vicious knife, whittling away at the bark of another branch.

Kalisa looks down the ladder, impressed at her father's ability to make simple twigs into sharp weapons. "Now, we only need a thousand more—give or take."

Martin agrees with a nod, stretching his arms to indicate the woods around them. "To survive in hostile environment, you must use what is available to gain an edge. You cannot win by giving the initiative to your enemy."

Martin throws the completed stick into the pile and stands up. Still holding his knife, he stretches and peers into the forest around them. "Whatever is coming, daughter, they are going to find two angry Rwandans waiting for them. I almost pity them."

Kalisa descends the ladder and hops down. She smiles reluctantly, testing the ground for a more in-depth conversation. "You've talked more in the last few days than I ever remember. It's good to hear your voice."

"Our past has made...finding things to talk about difficult."

Kalisa responds with a sarcastic chuckle. "Why is that? Just because I've been a drunken, gambling-addicted,

CHAPTER FIFTEEN

self-obsessed, cheating daughter, who has brought shame to your life?"

Martin bursts out laughing in a hearty and unrestrained cackle. He points his knife at her while flashing a playful grin. "It is good to know our weaknesses, even when they are so many."

There's an awkward silence, and Kalisa crosses her arms as she takes in the area around them. She looks back to Martin, hoping to keep the mood pleasant. "Dad, why didn't you ever remarry? You were young—still are young—enough to make a life with someone else?"

Martin lowers his eyes, but his voice is firm and honest. "Initially, I think it was the guilt I had for not being there when the attacks started. Your grandfather and I being away for work made the guilt unbearable."

"You both would've been dead like the rest if you'd stayed. Hacked apart and butchered. Nothing could have stopped those crowds."

Martin nods but regret still fills his features. "After the guilt and sorrow, I haven't been able to let your mother go. It's for the same reason that you sabotage your life with every chance you get. Such a horrid experience makes it difficult to have a normal relationship."

Looking sad, Kalisa nods. Hefting the trimmer, she ascends the ladder but stops halfway up. "Yeah, good point. Look what happens to someone who takes a chance to love a damaged person, like Rick."

Martin bends down and grabs another branch, moving back to his stump. He takes a moment to respond as he starts to strip away the crackling bark. "It is important to know, everything we do wrong can be forgiven. But you…we…have to let our present life have a chance. If we let the past win in our struggles, we will always lose."

Staring down at Martin, Kalisa's thoughts focus on the truth of his words. But truth and action are two different things; you can know every secret of life, but if you can't actually put them into practice, it really doesn't mean much. The world is full of people, rich and poor, who have roughly the same knowledge about living, but they end up in very different places if they don't actually follow through.

Nodding, Kalisa peers back above as she searches for the next branch to fashion into a dangerous weapon.

#

The yogurt shop is well-decorated, with images of kiddish dinosaurs and purple stars filling up the walls. A few people sit at small tables inside, chatting as they focus on their cold treats.

Rick stands in line, a Styrofoam cup of frozen chocolate yogurt held in his hand. Behind him is Seth, who waits for his turn to weigh his desert.

CHAPTER FIFTEEN

Paying for his small cup, Rick looks down at his son's monstrosity. In the bowl are a combination of yogurt, chocolate, sprinkles, caramel, and at least two kinds of crushed-up candy bars.

"Buddy, that is like three pounds of tastiness. Are you sure it'll be enough?"

Seth gives his dad a big grin, his eyes admiring the heart-stopping concoction. "Yeah, Dad, it's my favorite in the whole world."

Smiling, Rick places the bowl on the scale. After he gives the young cashier a bill, he motions to the front door. "I wish your favorite didn't always cost ten bucks a pop."

Stepping outside the yogurt shop, Rick and Seth walk at a relaxed pace on the sidewalk. To their side is a wide boulevard, and moderate traffic rushes past them under the streetlights of the early night. They are the only pedestrians in the area, and Seth's happy face is matched by his father's contented features while they stroll home.

As Rick licks at his melting yogurt, his eyes go cold. Looking across the street, he sees a large SUV parked, lonely and out-of-place in the gritty area. Its windows are tinted, allowing no view of what lies within. Stopping, Rick glares at the vehicle, wanting it gone by mere force of will. For several moments, he concentrates on its dark windshield in a one-sided staring contest.

Seth stops next to Rick, looking quizzically up at his dad as he chews.

DESPICABLE

From inside the vehicle, the curious gaze of the observer focuses on Rick. It sees father and son in a familiar green light, and the night provides no hindrance to its superior vision.

It waits, focusing intently.

Looking away, Rick begins walking up the street, and he pulls Seth close as they approach a crosswalk.

Leaning down, he whispers to Seth, while he sets down his yogurt on the dirty sidewalk. "Buddy, do me a favor and wait right here for a couple minutes. I'll be right back, I just gotta check on something. Alright?"

Seth looks confused, but he nods as he continues gnawing on the gooey mess.

With some suddenness, Rick changes direction back towards the yogurt shop. Breaking into a jog, he crosses the road by darting between two quickly slowing vehicles. As he comes up on the perpendicular road where his observer sits, Rick reaches under his loose-fitting shirt.

Drawing a small revolver as his quickens his pace, Rick creeps toward the dark SUV. As he gets close, the engine roars to life, and it speeds away from the curb down the side road.

Rick breathes hard from the exertion as he watches the vehicle accelerate away. He leans down, catching his breath and trying to hide the gun from obvious view. "You better run, dude."

Standing upright, he tucks the gun away and reverses course. Rushing back to Seth, he gets honked at by

CHAPTER FIFTEEN

pissed-off drivers as he as he makes his way back across the road.

When he gets back to his son, he speaks through labored breaths, pointing up the street. "Hey buddy, let's get back to grandma's…it's getting late."

Oblivious to the Drama, Seth waits for the walking signal to turn green as he slurps on the frozen goodness in his bowl. When the signal is clear, Rick shepherds Seth across the road, protectively glancing in every direction.

As the duo moves down the road into a more residential area, they are watched from another direction. Parked at the opposite corner of the intersection at a strip mall is a late-model sedan. A serious-looking man watches them move down the sidewalk through his rearview mirror. His eyes glow a peculiar yellow as he observes their shadows fade into the splotchy light of the neighboring street.

Chapter Sixteen

The inside of the cabin is clean and comfortable. Wooden walls and floors are complemented by sturdy handmade furniture, and a serving island constructed of a gorgeous oak stands next to a functional kitchen.

The ceiling soars above the large open room, and a loft with a comfortable bed faces the front of the living room. In the corner, away from the rear-facing kitchen, a small bathroom is equipped with a toilet and simple shower.

The front door stands open, and Martin reclines in a rocking chair on the weathered porch. He has a throw blanket over his legs, and a shotgun rests across his knees. Cradling a coffee cup, he scans the surrounding forest.

From the doorway, Kalisa stares out at her dad, a hopeful smile on her worried face. When it all comes down to it, she understands you can always rely on family—at least the one sitting outside.

DESPICABLE

Kalisa had always dealt with grief and self-imposed conflict due to the genocide, but just now she's also coming to terms with just how bad those events were on her father. He had his only son murdered in those events, as well as his dear wife. By all accounts, her mom and dad had a great marriage, and they were enjoying a life built from mutual trust and shared commitment. To have that stolen from you in a brief moment, and in turn, to only retain a deeply damaged daughter from the ordeal, is almost beyond comprehension. Add to that the rigors of emigration to a foreign culture and providing for what little family remained, and it's obvious to Kalisa that her father is a superhuman. *How did he make it without ever snapping and losing his mind?*

Turning around and filing away those thoughts, Kalisa strides to the kitchen, passing a bowl of chips and some uneaten sandwiches on the island countertop. A bottle of her father's favorite crappy American beer is also there, unopened for the moment.

Stopping at the stove, Kalisa looks down at several pans with bubbling dark liquids inside. She winces from the smell and moves to a back window, where she cracks the window to properly ventilate the confined interior.

On the counter next to her, her phone rings, and a smile cracks her face when she sees "Rick" as the caller.

"Hi…Rick…how are you?" Kalisa asks, her voice upbeat, despite the circumstances.

CHAPTER SIXTEEN

At Rick's mom's place, Rick leans against a ceramic counter. The room around him is dark, much like his dread-inducing tone of voice. "Hi. Are you and your dad alright?"

"Yeah. What's wrong? You sound weird."

"We were followed last night, some dark SUV, straight out of *Men in Black*," Rick says, and he tries to keep his voice low. "I think I chased 'em away, but I'm not sure what it means."

Kalisa's good mood melts away, and a panicked look fills her face. She decides in a moment a new course of action, hoping Rick will go along with her. "Rick, take your mom and Seth, and get out of there. I thought they were just after me, but—,"

"That's ridiculous, where are we gonna go? We'll be careful and call the cops if there's anything to worry about."

Walking to the couch in the living room, Kalisa peeks out the front door to be sure Martin doesn't hear. "Rick, please...please listen to me. I haven't earned it, but just trust me for now. Go to the airport and fly to your uncle's place in Georgia. Take your mom and Seth."

There's a pause from Rick's side, followed by concern creeping into his voice. "I don't have money for that. And what about work?"

"Borrow it any way you can. I'll pay you back later. And tell your work there's a family emergency. You're a

DESPICABLE

good employee; they'll work with you. Go, please. You've gotta move quickly."

Rick considers her words, staring into the dark kitchen as he mulls over their options. He nods cautiously. "Alright, we'll go. We'll pack a few bags and check for a flight at the airport. Should be safe if we stay in public."

Relieved, Kalisa leans into the phone, relaxing her iron grip on the case. The fear crawling up her throat recedes—at least for the moment. "Thank you and…I love you, Rick. Please tell Seth the same."

Rick doesn't answer her directly, but his words are kinder as he responds. "Kalisa, promise me you'll be careful. I'll call you when we get to Atlanta."

The line goes dead without further interaction. Kalisa straightens herself, moving to the front window. After peering into the midday light, her gaze moves to the coffee table, where her pistol lies waiting.

#

Mathias stands quietly in the back of the viewing room, looking ahead with well-rehearsed compassion. His features are rigid and without overt emotion, the image of a concerned professional.

Near the casket in front of him, a middle-aged female bawls and weeps with sweeping gestures of loss and pain. She leans over her deceased husband, raining kisses on

CHAPTER SIXTEEN

his dead face as she blubbers in hysterical gasps. Her long, mournful sobs drone on, like she's in competition to be the most distraught widow in existence.

A male relative steps up to guide her away from the corpse. Happy to avoid further practiced histrionics, the woman lets herself be comforted as she is led from the room.

As they exit the area, Mathias offers a polite and empathetic nod to the mourners. Ever the observant one, he catches the consoling man rolling his eyes at the display of emotional pain from the widow. *She should learn a thing or two about overacting; that really only ever worked for William Shatner.*

Struggling her way into the wider reception room, the widow sweeps the rest of the attendees with a "woe is me" gaze. She still comes across as upset, but those crocodile tears have subsided rather quickly.

Four female adults stand in front of a grieving crowd waiting under the mellow lights. The ladies must be close relatives of the decedent—perhaps daughters—and swap doubtful looks that can only be described as suspicious. The undercurrents of vague unrest in the gathering make it seem less a celebration than a horse race between warring family members.

Mathias watches the drama unfold without judgment or concern—the consummate death expert managing his domain on the way to the ever-after.

DESPICABLE

The widow restarts her tears and is consoled on the way out of the front door. As she crosses the threshold to the many waiting cars outside, it takes some time for the rest of the sad throngs to follow her out. Mathias waits with practiced empathy for the last of the relatives and well-wishers to exit.

When they've all departed, Mathias shakes his head and eases the door shut. He locks the various deadbolts, his lithe hands quickly securing the portal behind them.

Turning around, he sees Stefan, who steps from a shadowed area near the back door. The younger man shows some curiosity, then offers a considered frown. "That was quite a display of sorrow."

Mathias chuckles, shaking his head with an amused expression. "Wait until the will is read, and the sorrow will grow exponentially. The wife of two years will get most of the money. The old man was fabulously wealthy. He was bit of a baron in the local casino industry; he made killing off all those people least equipped to lose their own money. Of course, his family will sue—and surely lose in the subsequent litigation, burning up what little money he did leave them."

Surprised, Stefan stares at Mathias, like he's unsure if his boss is joking. Looking doubtful, he raises an eyebrow. "You can't know that."

"A lifetime of watching these matters play out…says that I can. Never underestimate greed or familial entitlement."

CHAPTER SIXTEEN

From the door leading to the preparation area, Kevin paces out. He stops short of coming too close to Mathias, obviously trying to be respectful. He adjusts his tie and tries to sound hopeful, even as sweat glistens on his too-big forehead. "The husband made contact with the woman. We were able to pinpoint her location from our contact at the telecom company."

Interested, Mathias cocks his head. "Where is she?"

Kevin takes out his phone, moving closer to Mathias. He holds the screen up and zooms in the focus to a forested region near "South Lake Tahoe." The location shows a vague road leading to a small lake, away from the much larger and more populated one. "There. She's back near that isolated lake. Only one way in that I can see…and not much else around there."

Mathias takes some time to absorb the information, and his expression moves from concentration to an intense scowl. Rubbing his clean-shaven face with his palm, he gestures toward the back of the building—where the cars are usually parked. "The anonymity of the area will be beneficial for our goals. I only hope we're not already too late. Get the vehicles ready and notify our best men. Make sure we are ready for any…eventualities."

Kevin nods and hurries back through the door. After he's gone, Mathias and Stefan make eye contact, but neither appears excited about what comes next.

#

Faint light from the fading day colors the sky above the deep forest, shrouding the cabin in shadows. Dusk has made the place seem decidedly more isolated, and visibility extends only a few feet back into the tree line and brush.

Kalisa stands on the porch, Licking her lips nervously. The darkness around her is almost complete, and she peers into the night, much like a helmsman peering from the prow of a ship on a forbidding sea.

Clanking from tools and metal being struck can be heard from inside the cabin, and Kalisa glances back into the unseen interior of the structure. Her frustration is palpable, and her voice rises appreciably. "Dad, I'm not sure how much time we got left. You have to hurry."

From inside, the sounds of construction stop. Martin's annoyed and fatigued voice drifts out from the silence. "If you had ever learned some meaningful skills like I suggested, like carpentry or welding, this would already be done. Instead of gambling and drinking…"

As Martin's voice drifts off, the clanging restarts, and Kalisa faces outward with a frown. Properly chastised, she grips her pistol in hand, flexing her fingers over the hardened plastic of its grip.

Lifting the weapon, she pans around the clearing in front of the house. Further out, the natural light from the darkening sky has entirely dissipated. In its place, the alternative illumination from a host of stars fails to reach all the way to the forest floor.

CHAPTER SIXTEEN

#

On the isolated road, the twists and turns of the pavement descend from an elevated mountain. Moonlight shines through scattered clouds, outlining the twisting highway visible over a long distance below.

Three SUVs drive, barreling down the grade, the cones of their powerful headlights probing the night ahead. Their engines roar with effort as they accelerate into the darkness, proceeding with little caution or regard for safety. Their speed and aggression are jarring, with the large vehicles taking the sharp corners in rapid turns. Their wheels squeal in protest, and their brake lights are rarely engaged.

At the bottom of the grade, the vehicles slow down, as if searching for something. Coming to crawl near the tree-lined edge of the forest, they stop completely, their engines idling. For a moment, there's only the silence of the surrounding woods to occupy the night.

In the front seat of the first vehicle, Stefan is nervous, and he glances back to Mathias. Mathias motions with his yellow eyes into the forbidding thickets.

Nodding, Stefan holds up a spotlight to illuminate the barely visible dirt path that Kalisa navigated earlier on her way to the cabin. The powerful light stabs into the isolated cover, showing clusters of brush and dense foliage around their simple route forward.

"Tell them to shut off their lights and go slowly," Mathias says, motioning to the accompanying vehicles. "We don't want to alert them, and they mustn't escape this time."

Stefan nods and keys the information over his mobile radio. Looking back to Mathias, his features are cold and determined in the dim light of the cab. "It's about five miles in."

The other SUVs gently move in front of Stefan's vehicle, taking point as they turn down that dirt road. The caravan moves cautiously as they bump through the blackness of the canopied forest.

As they roll ahead, they pass by an old pickup truck sitting near the vague pathway. The SUVs turn their lights out in unison, and the vehicles ease into the remote woods.

# #

From the loft at the far side of the cabin's interior, Kalisa peers down at the front door. The bed has been pulled to the edge of the latticed railing the runs the top of the sleeping space, and sandbags have been placed at the edge to protect the area.

Kalisa is sprawled on top of the bedding, her eyes sharp and expectant. Her pistol lies on a fluffy pillow to the side, while her dad's shotgun is perched next to it on the top of their sturdy sandbag protection. A box of

CHAPTER SIXTEEN

shotgun shells and several loaded magazines lie next to their weapons.

Kalisa glances over to her father. Martin dozes next to her, using the time to catch up on his rest. He leans against an old cushion with teddy bear decorations embroidered on its cover.

He snaps awake when she focuses on him, as if her wandering attention was enough to pull him from slumber. "We have no visitors yet?"

Kalisa smiles faintly and shakes her head. "Not yet. I don't know what we're gonna do if nobody comes."

"That is a bridge I would be happy to cross, daughter, but I fear we will be rewarded with company soon enough. If not today, then tomorrow. Soon, in any case."

Kalisa nods, glancing back down to the entrance. After some silence, she changes the subject. "Dad, if I don't make it, forgive me for all the bad shit I've done. And...help Rick with Seth. He's got a great dad, but Rick will have his hands full."

Martin thinks for a moment as his gaze moves from his daughter to the front door and back. A partial grin fills his face, and he places a weathered hand on her shoulder. "If you do not make it, you'll be in heaven with your brother and mom. If that's the case, I'll be envious."

Smiling, Martin leans over and kisses her on the head. It's the gesture of a concerned father she hasn't much experienced, and her heart hurts at the infrequency of the gesture. Her eyes tear up, and she wonders if there was ever a more perfect appreciation of humanity than the love that good parents feel for their offspring.

Quiet and contented for the moment, they stare down expectantly, not sure of what comes next.

Chapter Seventeen

Fifty yards from the front of the cabin, the hazy night vision of the creature focuses intently on the structure. Its enhanced sight watches for an extended period, scouring the windows and front door for any movement.

The creature by its nature is vicious and predatory, but it isn't brash to the point of being foolish. The thought of a meal is enticing, but as with all its conquests, it must be wary as it corners its prey. The world rarely rewards hunters, even savage and strong ones, with long lives if they are stupid.

No movement finds its attention. They must be sleeping.

Creeping from the tree line, the creature scans the area carefully as it approaches the cabin. Kalisa's vehicle is parked ahead, along with piles of branches and twigs scattered around the front yard.

Something catches the beast's attention. At various points on the ground are breaks in the soil, where different temperatures are noticeable amongst the upturned earth. The closer to the cabin, the more these holes are evident, made to ensnare an aggressor.

The creature lowers itself, slipping its clawed hand into one of the holes. In that space are several sharpened stakes, pointed upward

DESPICABLE

to maim a careless attacker. The edge of the creature's claw scrapes the end of the sharpened stick.

Stepping away from the trap, the creature moves closer to the building, more vigilant with each approaching step. The rest of the snare holes are easily avoidable, and the pulse of the beast quickens as it anticipates its upcoming meal.

It stops in front of the porch, arching its head to take in its surroundings. The distant thump of a heartbeat comes to its hearing, following by the intermittent beat of another person. Both of its victims are inside. BOTH are awake, as their heightened pulses give them away. The anticipation of its upcoming kill fills the creature with a longing, the kind that only be quenched by torn flesh and fresh, pumping blood.

The creature tenses its legs, ready to finally end the chase. With a rush, it launches itself at the door.

#

The creature crashes into the well-lit front room, easily breaking through the front door. It skids onto a rug on the inside floor...and drops straight through it.

As it lands on the ground below, its clawed feet and legs are impaled on sharp metal rods. The rods have metal spikes welded at angles to it, so they act as barbs when they stab into flesh. The creature is hopelessly stuck in the barbed crawl space that Martin has fashioned from the area underneath the cabin's regular floor.

CHAPTER SEVENTEEN

The beast itself is a bizarre nightmare to see in the light of the room. Its head and face look vaguely human, except for the mottled dark skin pulled tight around its lips and eyes. Its mouth is full of sharp teeth, teeth that appear too large for any practical use. Its eyes flash anger and hatred from their yellow orbs.

The rest of the monster is weird, as it is dressed in seemingly normal work overalls. Its arms are clothed in a short-sleeve shirt but appear too long for its frame as they flail around. Its hands are topped by black claws that are inches long and deadly sharp, and they scrape the wooden floor as they try to find purchase to drag itself free.

The animal-like being screams a high-pitched bellow as it struggles against its brutal metal trap. It bangs and wrenches against its shackles, tearing out chunks of its own flesh as it tries to break out.

"What the fuck is that?" shouts Kalisa, and she moves her arm in down motion to her father. "Do it, now."

Martin reaches to his side, where he cranks down an improvised metal lever.

Two metal plates move from the side of the pit below, moving into the abdomen of the creature. Below the plates are more spikes pointed at an angle. As the creature roars and rages against the thick metal, the spikes holding it in place are driven further into its stomach. It's a vicious and effective restraint for the grotesque creature.

Martin and Kalisa share disbelieving stares, not understanding who or what it could be. In shock, they are unable to move, even as the wails of their intruder continue.

Snapping free of his fright, Martin motions down to the creature. "I'll finish it off."

Rising, Martin slings his shotgun on his shoulder and climbs down the loft's ladder. Exasperated, Kalisa doesn't know what to do, but she comes back to her senses as he reaches the bottom. She stands, panning her weapon around the room in a protective gesture.

Shouldering the shotgun, Martin leans close to the flailing beast, preparing to blow its head apart.

A crash comes from the side window, and the flash of another creature lunges into the room. Moving distressingly fast, it bashes into Martin, sending him reeling against the log wall of the cabin. His head cracks against the hard surface, and he slumps to the floor, limp and unmoving.

"Dad," screams Kalisa and she levels her pistol, pulling the trigger as fast as it will allow. Her bullets slam into the new creature, forcing it back against the wall. Black blood erupts from its wounds as she fires center mass into the beast, and more blood peppers the surface behind as several bullets pass through the predator.

The creature slides down the wall, mortally wounded from a dozen direct hits. Out of bullets, Kalisa drops her magazine and clambers down the ladder. Moving quickly, she stuffs a new clip into the weapon, racking the slide forward with an authoritative SCHIIK.

CHAPTER SEVENTEEN

Striding to the creature, she holds out the pistol to deliver the Coup De Grace. With a rush, the creature comes alive and spins to the side, moving along the wall as Kalisa quick-fires several more shots into the wood behind it.

Spinning about, the creature launches itself off the wall, jumping toward Kalisa. Two of its razor claws sink into Kalisa's thigh, and she screams in agony as she backpedals, trying to keep it off her. She fires several more shots into the creature's chest, and it convulses with each blast of the 9-millimeter weapon.

With an inhuman twist and push, the creature throws Kalisa across the room, where she thuds into the kitchen counter and collapses into a heap. Grunting, she tries to pull herself up. She makes it to one knee, but her hands are now empty—her pistol lost in the violence.

The injured creature focuses on her, and a grin makes its terrifying and bloody face even more wicked. Straightening itself, the creature moves toward Kalisa. It throws a table aside with a crash as its confident gaze fixes on its inevitable victim.

With a flick of her hand, Kalisa casts a pan of liquid on the creature's face. The boiling acid sizzles on the beast, and the creature bellows as it claws at the burning substance. Unable to brush the liquid free, its shrieks are intense and panicked.

A frightful boom fills the room, and Kalisa holds out her borrowed bear revolver toward the wailing monster.

The thunderclap of several more shots emanate from the weapon, and huge chunks are blown from the creature with each enormous bullet. Stepping as close as she dares, Kalisa steadies the gun to aim with her last round.

The final crack of the weapon matches the creatures head disappearing from its shoulders, and chunks of its brains are blown throughout the room. The rest of the body collapses with a sickly thud.

Grimacing from pain, Kalisa gently re-holsters her revolver into the small of her back. The fury of the moment keeps her moving, and she kicks the dead creature several times, screaming in agonized triumph. "Got you, you motherfucker."

The room is suddenly quiet, and the trapped beast to the side looks up to Kalisa, its hateful stare moving between her and its dead comrade.

Kalisa meets the beast's gaze and tilts her head. *Well, what do we have here?*

A vengeful smile breaks out across Kalisa's features, and her eyes move to the corner of the room. The creature follows her gaze, a hint of worry in its unnatural demeanor. Stumbling over, Kalisa grabs and hefts a baseball bat that was leaning against the wall.

The remaining creature carefully watches Kalisa as she approaches, and it stops struggling against its pointed bonds. Appearing to accept its fate, the hatred leaves it eyes. Something like acceptance is just visible in its distant stare as it awaits Kalisa's justice.

CHAPTER SEVENTEEN

Kalisa slams the bat into the monster's thick skull, braining it with a brutal crack. She begins to shout as she hits it over and over, bellowing words between each smack of the bat.

"I…want…a…fucking…life. I…need…a…fucking…life."

Each smash of the blunt weapon into the beast's head breaks apart its skull. Gore, bone, and brains are flung around the room as she whacks it again and again. After a score of blows, the head is pulverized into smashed gristle.

Stopping, Kalisa remembers her father and shouts out as she spins to him. "Dad."

Throwing aside the bat, she rushes to Martin's side at the far wall. Sliding down next to her dad, she straightens him up and checks for a pulse. Finding a steady heartbeat, she smiles and gives Martin a frantic hug. Tears of thankful joy flood down her cheeks as she quietly thanks God.

Glancing up, Kalisa takes in the room around her, and she's repulsed by the carnage. Blood and bits of flesh are everywhere, making it look like a lawnmower was let loose in a slaughterhouse. A strange thought crosses her mind: *This is gonna be a hell of a cleanup.*

From the broken window, a hand reaches in, followed by the figure of yet another creature, dressed in those same shitty work overalls. Bigger than the others, it steps carefully into the cabin, its yellow-eyed gaze stopping on each of its dead companions. Surprise and anger mix together in those evil eyes, and the beast focuses on Kalisa.

It advances toward her, ready to end the contest once and for all.

Kalisa knows it will now finish her; she has no delusions about surviving another encounter with such a menace. A feeling of resigned peace fills her inside, and she smiles at the approaching beast. "I'm coming home, momma."

From the front door, another figure emerges, hopping past the trap door and mangled beast in the trap. It's…Ben? Her special large friend from work. Except, he doesn't look the same. His face is angular and ferocious, with sharp teeth that take up too much of his mouth.

Ben faces the incoming creature, grunting a challenge to the similar-looking beast. The creature looks hesitant for a moment, taking a measure of the former security guard. Tensing itself, it leaps toward Ben in a savage attack.

Ben catches the creature with frightening speed by the neck. He holds it at arm's length while the beast slashes at his exposed arms, leaving gaping gashes down Ben's hardened skin.

With a grunt, Ben heaves it up and inverts the creature, bringing it crashing down on its head. He

CHAPTER SEVENTEEN

smashes it several more times into the floorboards, smacking it with a final sickening crunch.

The creature goes limp, and Ben lets it fall to the ground. Placing a steel-toed boot on its head, Ben stomps down, crunching it into a broken collection of shattered skull fragments and mushy gore.

Kalisa sits in shock and watches the contents of the creature's head leak onto the floorboards. Thinking she's dreaming, she raises her eyes to Ben.

Ben looks down at her, and his face is normal again, with no sharp teeth or viciousness. "Hi, Kalisa, I've missed you."

He doesn't sound developmentally disabled now; in fact, Kalisa has never heard a more rational or lucid person in her life. As she continues to stare at him, his image starts to get a little fuzzy. Looking down at her wounded leg, she places her hand over it, trying to staunch the blood loss.

Growing dizzier, Kalisa tries to talk, but only an incoherent sigh escapes her lips. Ben moves toward her, and she reaches up for his hand.

Darkness overcomes her.

In Kalisa's dream, she is reliving the same event in her long-distant home in Rwanda. It is still night outside, and moonlight floods into her home through austere windows and the open front door.

DESPICABLE

Kalisa crouches in the hidden basement of her simple home, watching slivers of light enter the space through the floorboards above her. The terrified young girl squints, seeing the figure of the man who hacked to death the person that drug out her family's corpses.

The figure stands in the shadows of the unlit home, panning his head around in search of something. His bloody machete is held at the ready, as if expecting new victims to be in the area. He shifts his weight as he waits for something.

Breathing hard, Kalisa trembles with fear as she tries to make out the man's features. He is just out of view, even as she watches drops of blood fall from his weapon in the night's soft light. As the moments pass, she shifts her weight and stifles a groan of pain from the horrible wound to her back.

The man hovering above notices, and he lowers his eyes to the floor. An errant ray of moonlight finally illuminates his face, revealing the man who saved her so long ago.

#

Kalisa's eyes flip open, and she blinks several times, trying to get her bearings on the cabin floor. Focusing ahead, she sees Mathias Baudin, crouching on his haunches directly in front of her. He wears a self-effacing grin, one that is friendly and inquisitive. He doesn't say anything as he continues his careful analysis of Kalisa's confused face.

"It…was you," whispers Kalisa, and she struggles with her emotions. "How's that possible?"

CHAPTER SEVENTEEN

Mathias lets the silence linger a bit longer before he speaks. He is happy, of that there's no doubt, but he's also looking for something as he stares deep into her eyes. It's as if he's evaluating her soul, not just her physical or mental condition.

"We really have to quit meeting like this, Kalisa. Saving your life is becoming a bit of a habit. A pleasant habit perhaps, but a monotonous one just the same."

Kalisa raises herself on the wall so she can get a better look around. Stefan stands near to the broken window, watching her intently, while other men are busy cleaning the area. Some have brushes and scrub the various splotches of blood, while others are collecting pieces of flesh into plastic bags.

"My father?" asks Kalisa, panic rising as she straightens herself. She grimaces from the pain in her bandage-wrapped leg.

"Outside, and I'm told in satisfactory health. My men have looked him over thoroughly."

Kalisa relaxes, relief washing over her features.

"I was in Rwanda," continues Mathias, keeping his good-guy grin. "I left there after my work was done. After we could do our part in that hideous time."

"But you haven't aged," says Kalisa, trying to grasp what's going on. "It's been almost three decades, and you're still…the same. It's not possible."

Mathias grins even wider. "Life is full of things that aren't possible, yet they happen nevertheless. I've been alive longer than this country. Several times more, in fact."

Kalisa doesn't respond, and the silence is only broken by the sounds of scrubbing brushes and pacing feet as men enter and exit.

The lack of a response urges Mathias to continue. "We are a race not unlike humans. We have the same emotions, desires…and weaknesses. But we count our lives in centuries, not decades."

Mathias rises from his crouch and moves to an overturned chair. Reversing it, he straddles the wooden stool, keeping his focus on Kalisa. "Unfortunately, we have certain…dietary considerations. We can only live like we do if we eat people."

Visibly upset, Kalisa tries to rise completely from her wounded stupor. She makes it all the way to her feet but has to lean against the wall to keep her balance.

"No, no. We only eat the dead—at least, most of us," Mathias says, holding up his hands in a non-threatening gesture.

Looking down, Mathias moves his attention to the creature Ben killed. He frowns, not hiding his contempt for it. "There are those among us that stray from the safe path. Take feeding into their own hands."

Mathias motions to the slain creature, a distasteful frown on his face. "And they must be destroyed. Untreated human meat drives them insane. They look human and can hold basic jobs…but the urge to feed and

CHAPTER SEVENTEEN

hunt overwhelms their rational side. They look for wars and violent conflict to allow them to feast as much as their sick inclinations will allow. It's not good for them, but they cannot stop. It also opens our kind up to undue attention, which we cannot allow."

Covering her face with her hand, Kalisa tries to emerge from her off-kilter dizziness. She whispers through her hand as she struggles to understand. "You feed on people? Like my grandfather?"

"Not him. You were adamant that he not be cremated. We burn animals to swap the ashes with the deceased, allowing a ready supply of meat for our kind. It's easier to do in current times…people are cremated more often. There are fewer religious objections."

Ben returns to the cabin through the front door, flashing a warm smile at Kalisa. Mathias gets his attention and motions to the corpse of the last creature killed.

Ben nods and goes outside, where he retrieves a tarp amongst a pile of plastic bags. Coming back inside, he unfurls the plastic next to the body of the beast he killed.

Quite cheerful, he throws the remains on the tarp. As he bends down to arrange the body for transport, he meets Kalisa's eyes. "You were always so kind to me, and you never had to be. These things are often noticed in this world, Kalisa, even if you don't realize it."

Folding the plastic around his dead enemy, Ben easily hefts it over his shoulder, exiting the room with an airy and pleasant mood.

DESPICABLE

Perplexed and not knowing what to think, Kalisa looks back to Mathias. "You said treated meat? How…?"

"With the same method we've used for millennia," replies Mathias, and he withdraws a vial of the glowing green goo from his coat. "You've seen it before, at my business."

Kalisa nods, remembering the big jar of crap where they treat the bodies in the preparation room. The thought of that being some kind of special sauce for immortality is less than appealing, and she cringes at the thought of eating dead people bathed in the stuff.

Standing, Mathias moves to the kitchen, where he peers down at a pan of the acid that Kalisa was making before the attack. He nods at it with respect for her ingenuity. "When one of our kind is eating…unclean food, they can get the scent of prey, and they are never able to let it go. This can cause even more problems for us."

"Those fucking monsters followed me from Africa. From almost thirty years?"

Mathias nods, turning to Kalisa with that same smile, the one that shows he'll always be your best friend. It's a look that makes Kalisa profoundly uneasy.

"The ones that escaped me in Rwanda, yes. They took the opportunity of ethnic strife to feed openly, murdering with no regard for our unique status. So, we had to intervene, sending people from all over the world to exterminate the threat. Unfortunately, some got away."

CHAPTER SEVENTEEN

Mathias walks close to Kalisa, lowering his voice a bit. "And so, we had to draw them out, make sure the last of them were hunted down. We...appreciate your cooperation at being our bait."

Finding her courage, Kalisa stares at Mathias, keeping her voice low. "You can't get away with this. Somebody will find out."

Mathias shows Kalisa a patronizing and smug expression. "Did you ever notice that wherever you are, morticians and funeral homeowners are creepy?"

Kalisa blinks, confused.

Mathias grins, but there's an unmistakably cold edge to his voice... "Now you know why that is. We have the money and political power to solve most problems...and other options if something more is required. Like with your police boyfriend."

Kalisa gulps, thinking about Lance and his disappearance. Her concern is palpable—for her and her family. "Why tell me any of this?"

The area around them is almost clean, at least as much as could be expected, considering the recent and very violent past. Mathias nods to Stefan and two of his workers, and they exit the cabin with the last of the fight's debris.

Kalisa and Mathias are now alone.

"I tell you so that you can know the stakes if you should feel the need to divulge anything," Mathias says, his eyes growing deadly serious. "To anyone. You are never out of our reach—wherever you may be."

Kalisa stays quiet, gulping at the threat. Suddenly, Seth and Rick don't seem particularly safe—even in Georgia. Or perhaps Siberia for that matter.

Returning to a pleasant smile, Mathias changes his tone to an upbeat and happy mode. "I wish you well, Kalisa, you are a hard-nosed and very enterprising woman. Please contact me if you ever feel the need. You don't know it, but you now have friends in very high places. As long as you treat them—us—as friends."

Turning around, Mathias strides from the cabin and walks to one of the black SUVs in front. As he climbs in, Kalisa hobbles to the doorway.

Her dad stands up from the steps, where he's been watching the bizarre cleanup. He has a bloody bandage wrapped around his head but is otherwise unhurt. He appears in good spirits—considering the circumstances.

Martin fixes his daughter with a confused gaze as Mathias and his men pull away from the cabin. "Daughter, would you tell me what in God's name just happened?"

Chapter Eighteen

Rick peers into his bathroom mirror, evaluating himself under the bright light of the dead-bug-filled lamp on the ceiling. Dressed in a sweater and jeans, he pokes at dark circles under his eyes, wondering what happened to that boyish face that used to return the stare.

Rick doesn't much like what he sees, as he's caught in that curious stage of life where he can still pass for young amongst middle-aged people—but can also be seen as a shriveled old man by people in their twenties.

Deciding he doesn't really care, for now, Rick shrugs away his doubts and smiles. He flashes a grin and continues his self-appraisal, focusing on his healthy teeth. *At least those could still look good when I'm an old bastard.*

Stepping out of the bathroom, Rick walks to the front of the house, where he stares into the kitchen. Moving to the refrigerator, there's a moment of indecision as his gaze sweeps across several boxes of cereal. Reaching into a cabinet, he withdraws an enormous bowl, one that looks like it could be used to mix meals for a whole family—or a small village.

Rick dumps an entire box of cornflakes into the cavernous bowl, then tops it with a generous heap of sugar from a container on the counter. Unbowed, he grabs a half-gallon of milk from the fridge and completes the gourmet endeavor by emptying most of it over the simple meal.

A grin forms on his face, and Rick balances the food as he moves into the living room. Taking his place on the couch, he scoops up a spoonful and smacks with delight.

The TV catches his attention, and Rick raises the volume between chewing. On the screen, an old male newscaster drones on:

"The police have indicated the missing officer has moved to another locale and is accounted for. His police equipment has been returned, and no further action is expected in this bizarre missing person's case..."

Rick kills the sound with the remote and tosses it on the coffee table, his mood souring. "You won't be missed, asshole."

Saying that aloud and to himself somehow makes Rick feel better, and he reassumes his good mood as he digs back in. Nothing like cereal and TV on a Saturday afternoon to make a grown man happy.

CHAPTER EIGHTEEN

A knock on the front door gets Rick's attention, and his mood falters again as he moves to the door. Easing it open, he nods at a chubby delivery driver.

"Rick Price?" asks the disinterested man, and he hands Rick a pad to sign for the delivery.

Rick is offered a small, wrapped box, and he returns to the living room with a perplexed stare. Opening the box, he withdraws a set of car keys, along with a note. The note is written in Kalisa's flowing penmanship, with each word precise and neat:

Rick,
Look out front. South Tahoe campground, your favorite space.
-Kalisa and Seth

Moving back out the door, Rick walks to the middle of the driveway. Surprised, his eyes and mouth lock open.

Parked on the curb is an immense diesel truck, sparkling and brand new. Attached to it is a clean fifth-wheel trailer, also new and shiny. A red bow is tied around the front of the vehicle, looking like a much larger version of a child's Christmas present.

#

The fire pit is filled with coals, burning gently in the crisp mountain air. A rack of glazed meat roasts on the top of the licking flames, skewered and expertly arranged to bring pink marinated beef to culinary perfection.

Kalisa stares down at the delectable meat, letting its heavenly aroma soak into her very being. Breathing it in, she looks to the side, where a hungry Seth is also engaged in food worship.

"You think he'll come?" asks Kalisa, and her features become defensive. "You don't think I'm putting it on too thick?"

Seth scrunches his nose as he considers her words. Shrugging, he glances up to look at the surrounding campground. A few yards away are several elegant, white-sheeted tables: One is made with up with expensive china and champagne glasses, while the others are full of all manner of delectable foods, from pastries to aromatic soups.

A chef stands to the side, working from his own small serving table. The white-clad cook hovers over his preparations, gently slicing cooked vegetables and herbs.

Near the chef, a 5-star waiter is also dressed in fine clothing and standing at attention. Picking at his tight collar, the groomed professional appears uncomfortable and out of place in the dusty camping area.

From a distance, the low rumble of a diesel truck fills the air. The rest of the camping area is deserted, and the incoming sound of the humming engine makes it seem like an aircraft is inbound. Seth and Kalisa look at each other with hopeful eyes.

The huge truck and its attached trailer emerge over a small hill, its breaks and carriage squeaking as it eases into

CHAPTER EIGHTEEN

view. Coming to a stop near mother and son, it takes a considerable time for the vehicle to align itself properly with their campsite.

Rick emerges from the truck's cab, caution and wonder on his face. He walks slowly towards his wife and son, glancing in awe at the food and workers.

Snapping into action, the waiter paces to the table, where he pulls a chair back in preparation for the dinner guests. The chef also moves quickly, striding to the fire, where he begins to slice beef for the main course.

Rick stops short, not knowing what to do or say. In answer, Kalisa embraces him, throwing her arms around his shoulders and clutching him close. Seth joins the duo in a hug around both of their waists.

"Wha…How on earth could you afford this?" asks Rick.

Facing the other way, Kalisa half-giggles, half-cries into Rick's ear. Warm and intense emotions fill her words, and for once, she appreciates everything she has. "I finally…got lucky."

As Kalisa smiles joyfully, her teary eyes flash a strong shade of yellow.

The End

About the Author

Tim lives in Nevada, where he makes a life enjoying all things horror and thriller-related, from films to books, and even the occasional convention. He has three children, two cats, and he enjoys providing reading entertainment for the monster and creature-loving masses.

If you like this novel, he would appreciate a review or a follow on Facebook:
https://www.facebook.com/Horrorthrillerguy

or

https://www.horrorthrillerguy.com

For the opportunity to win free hardcover versions of this and all future books, please join his mailing list:
https://mailchi.mp/143ae89c5418/horrorthrillerguy

Also by Timothy Bryan:
Chindi
https://www.amazon.com/dp/B09FSCS87K

The Huntsman of Corvinus
https://www.amazon.com/dp/B09J8R5XFJ

Made in United States
North Haven, CT
16 August 2022